I0578020

THE MIRROR MAN

A THRILLER

MARK ST. GERMAIN

THE MIRROR MAN

Copyright © 2022 by Mark St. Germain

All rights reserved.

Published by Ibis Books, 2349 Hyde Park Street, Sarasota, FL, 34239.

No part of this book may be reproduced in any form or by any electronic or mechanical means, including information storage and retrieval systems, without written permission from the author, except for the use of brief quotations in a book review.

This is a work of fiction. All of the characters, organizations, locations, and events portrayed in this novel are either products of the author's imagination or are used fictitiously.

Mark St. Germain asserts the moral right to be identified as the author of this work.

Mark St. Germain has no responsibility for the persistence or accuracy of URLs for external or third-party Internet Websites referred to in this publication and does not guarantee that any content on such Websites is, or will remain, accurate or appropriate.

Designations used by companies to distinguish their products are often claimed as trademarks. All brand names and product names used in this book and on its cover are trade names, service marks, trademarks, and registered trademarks of their respective owners. The publishers and the book are not associated with any product or vendor mentioned in this book. None of the companies referenced within the book have endorsed the book.

First edition

ISBN-13: 978-1-956672-00-8 (Paperback edition)

ISBN-13: 978-1-956672-01-5 (Ebook edition)

For Paul, my brother

STORIES TAKE FLIGHT AT IBIS BOOKS

STORIES FOR READERS, RESOURCES FOR WRITERS

The IBIS is sacred to Thoth, the Egyptian god of learning,
inventor of writing, and scribe to the gods.

They are gregarious birds that live, travel, and breed in flocks.

And they are legendary for their courage.

ibis-books.com

"To put oneself in another's place, to see things from his perspective, is to imagine something that has never happened."

- *THE SELF AS FANTASY: FANTASY AS THEORY,*
  WILLIAM I. GROSSMAN, M.D.

I saw a shadow touch a shadow's hand
On Bleecker Street

- *BLEECKER STREET,* JERRY LANDIS AND
  PAUL SIMON

OWEN MOSER CUT A HARD RIGHT, VEERING OFF COUNTY Highway 27 and onto the rutted dirt road of Trinity Pass, driving fast as his cruiser's springs would allow.

He had spotted the fire a half-mile ahead. This far from town, there were more fields than farmhouses. The flames in the distance were the only light visible in the chill October night.

The seven volunteers of the Franklin Fire Department were already at work spraying down the small home. Owen braked to a stop beside the Fire Truck and made his way to Fire Chief Charlie Stone. He shouted to be heard over the flames hissing as the water hit them.

"Is everybody out?" Moser called.

"Don't know," Stone answered, his eyes still on the fire. "Can't get in to see."

"Should be parents and two kids," Moser told him.

But Stone was already moving away, shouting instructions to his men.

Moser watched until he found himself shielding his eyes, not from the light of the flames, but a beam of light bouncing off his police car mirror. He turned, facing in the direction it came from, but there was nothing to see but dark woods.

Moser walked toward the trees after taking a flashlight from his car. Crunching through the fall leaves, he stopped, spotting an object in the undergrowth before him: a stuffed animal. He picked it up, a one-eyed, potbellied bear, his fur scarce from being gripped, dragged, hugged.

He heard a small gasp: the sound of someone inhaling, trying to hold their breath.

Moser trained his flashlight on the forest ahead, first at ground level, then higher and higher still.

There: a treehouse. And staring down at him from it, two boys in pajamas. Owen had seen both kids in town but didn't know their names. Peggy would. His wife, a teacher at Franklin Elementary, hadn't forgotten a student's name in the eleven years she'd been teaching.

Michael and Justin Ash, ages eight and five.

Releasing his breath, Justin let out a sob. Michael, though, stared back steadily, meeting Moser's eyes.

Moser walked closer, holding up the bear for the boys to see.

"This guy looks scared," he said. "Maybe one of you should come down and hold him."

Justin climbed down eagerly, too fast for Michael to stop him. Only when Justin reached the ground did Michael descend and take his brother's hand. Justin reached out for his stuffed bear with the other.

Moser walked them out of the woods and stopped at his car. Michael still gripped Justin's hand tightly, as if he'd never let go.

The fire had won, Moser noted. The house looked like a bonfire, not a home. Justin stared, fascinated, too astonished to realize his toys, clothes, and his life up to now were gone.

"You ever drive?" Moser asked him. Justin said nothing. Moser walked the boy to his Ford, opening the driver's door.

"Let's flash some lights." He leaned in, flipping the switch for the rotating cherry light on top of the vehicle. He turned to help the boy into the car but felt resistance. Michael Ash wouldn't let his brother's hand go.

"You're the big guy," Moser told him. "You can help me figure some things out."

Distracted, Michael allowed Justin to yank his hand free. Moser lifted the smaller boy, placing him behind the steering wheel, and then put his hand on the older brother's shoulder.

"Let's give him some room," Moser suggested.

Michael still watched his brother, even as Moser led him toward the fire truck.

"Were your mom and dad home with you tonight?" No response. "Where are they?" He stooped to see Michael's face, noticing his bare feet. "Do you know how the fire started? Son, I need you to talk to me."

Gently, Moser lifted the boy's chin.

"It's important. Is someone in there?"

In the years after, when Moser looked back on the moment, he never forgot the boy's face. His eyes empty, his face impassive, and then a change, a shift of the boy's expression to one of alertness, expectation, and, finally, worry—the reaction he was hoping for, the same as his own.

All this in the moment before they heard the shout of a fireman: *"Get the boy!"*

Moser turned to see Justin running toward the fiery house faster than he thought a five-year-old could move.

"JUSTIN!"

Michael's scream pierced Moser, costing him a moment of response.

Michael sped toward his brother, who had already

vanished in the smoky haze. Moser and Chief Stone caught up with them only when Michael had dragged Justin backward through the smoke. The younger boy was reaching down for an object covered with fall leaves.

When the men arrived, Michael threw his arms around Justin. Moser looked up, hearing the screech of splintering wood over the sounds of the fire.

He scooped Michael up under one arm as Chief Stone carried Justin, and they ran until they outdistanced the dark gusts of smoke. A charred plaster wall released its hold on the chimney, bricks and boards crashing to the ground.

Putting Michael and Justin down, Moser sucked cool air into his lungs before turning back to look. What once had been home now was a pile of charred wood, brick, and fire.

"Chief!" Bud Kelton ran toward Stone, his face blackened by soot that couldn't hide his red rush of adrenalin. "We found the parents."

Moser caught Kelton's eye, indicating the children's presence. Michael had taken Justin's hand again. Moser would remember that, too, and the eight-year-old's fury when they later tried to separate them.

Moser guided the men a few steps farther from the young brothers.

"First floor, in the back," Kelton continued, oblivious to anything but his find. "Both of 'em in bed."

"They never tried to get out?" Stone asked.

Even before Kelton replied, Moser anticipated his answer's chill.

"Couldn't get far with their skulls smashed in."

Moser looked back at the children as an ambulance braked to a stop behind them, its siren winding down. It was Michael's face that held him, Michael staring back at him, the boy's expression first one of disbelief, then revulsion, and finally a stunned sorrow.

Had he heard what Kelton said even through the siren's wail?

He must have, Moser thought. What other explanation could there be for the boy's reactions, so clearly reflecting his own?

Michael held his gaze. It was Moser who broke contact, distracted by a red stream on Michael's slender arm. He's cut, Moser thought. A step closer and he saw it: the object Justin had seized from the lawn, now clutched in his left hand as tightly as Michael held his right.

A baseball bat, a Louisville Slugger, its tip and barrel liquid red, dripping down the handle onto dying fall leaves.

"Sweet Jesus."

Moser heard Chief Stone's murmur as he stared at Michael. Michael stared back, his face vacant of emotion, his eyes fastened on Moser's, searching for a clue how to feel.

THERE WERE DAYS, TOO MANY, WHEN DR. HENRY Granville wondered whether the doctors or the patients contributed more to the ulcer he developed administrating Bunyon Psychiatric Hospital in Hawley, Indiana.

Today, there was no contest.

Standing before his desk, Dr. Maureen Cherry and Dr. Ronald Larkin continued their argument that had already raged for weeks through reports and emails.

"Michael Ash hasn't left this hospital in over twenty years," Dr. Larkin insisted. "Not once. And that was his choice."

"Then isn't that even more reason to support, even cele- brate that he wants to leave now?" Dr. Cherry countered.

"To live in a halfway house with minimal security-"

"A fully supervised group home with trained staff."

"*Trained?* Oh, yes, I'd forgotten. Their B.A.'s qualify them to serve fast food and babysit sociopaths."

Dr. Granville fought an impulse to swing around in his chair and put his back to them both. Only yesterday he'd noticed that the Maple tree outside his second-story window had traded half its green leaves for red.

Not yet thirty, Dr. Cherry was one of his youngest staff

members, the word "young" normally used to describe anyone shy of sixty-five. Attractive enough in the outside world, among the hospital's staff, she had risen to the rank of Goddess. Six-foot, shoulder-length black hair, first-class cheekbones, and intense blue eyes, especially when sparked with anger, now the case.

Dr. Cherry's adversary was Dr. Ronald Larkin, a staff member so senior he was said to be inked into the institution's ground plans. His age only underlined the incongruity of Dr. Larkin's hairpiece, a jet-black sphere resembling a beanie with bangs.

Larkin was not the first psychiatrist, Dr. Granville mused, that he knew with a facial tick. In any other profession, he wondered, would such a quirk be ignored? A dentist with green teeth? A chiropractor who winced every time he bent over?

There, again: Dr. Larkin's involuntary grimace, lifting the left side of his face, gone as quickly as it came.

"Michael Ash has been here since he was eight years old. He's spent over two-thirds of his life in this hospital," Dr. Granville said.

"He's lucky he didn't spend that time in jail," Dr. Larkin countered. "The jury must have been as low functioning as he is. The boy killed both his parents. Brutally."

"In self-defense! The jury knew, as well as you, that his parents abused him," Dr. Cherry insisted, all civility abandoned. "You do know that, don't you? You treated him for how many years?"

The unspoken word "unsuccessfully" flashed through all their heads as if lit in neon.

"I've treated him intermittently since he came here," Dr. Larkin conceded. "Which is why I dispute your wrongheaded, and, frankly, puerile diagnosis. Even on his best days, Ash is still antisocial and uncommunicative. And every day, he's contemptuous of authority."

"Contemptuous? Because he mimics your tic?"

She said it, Dr. Granville thought, impressed. She's named the unnamable. It is far less embarrassing for an Emperor to be told he's wearing no clothes than a therapist to be informed he has an uncontainable response to stress.

"I've read through your files on Michael," Dr. Cherry continued. "Not only were your sessions unproductive, but they're inadequately documented."

"My reports don't change because he never has. Every session he sat glaring at me, answering caustically, if at all. He's never felt guilt, not even a twinge of regret for killing his parents. Michael Ash is an amoral individual. He can't differentiate between right and wrong. He doesn't have the tools to."

"I disagree," Dr. Cherry maintained. "And now, finally, when Michael is making progress, you want to keep him incarcerated here."

"Thank you, Doctors," Dr. Granville interrupted. Both turned to him in a silent appeal for support.

"Dr. Cherry, I have your report and recommendations. Dr. Larkin, I have your letter of protest. I'll consider both and then get back to you."

"Thank you," Dr. Cherry responded. She hesitated, uncertain what more to say, then left the room, closing the door behind her.

Dr. Larkin patted his hairpiece as if to be sure he had at least one ally with him.

"Can I be blunt?" he asked.

Can you be anything but, Dr. Granville wondered?

"You and I have had our differences, Henry. I'm sure you see me as an arrogant, old-school son of a bitch. But that doesn't make me a son of a bitch who's wrong. Michael Ash's 'breakthrough,' as she'd have you believe, is the textbook reflexive transference of a narcissistic personality disorder. But, in Ash's case, the transference is reversed: instead of him seeing his personality manifested in his therapist, he's assuming hers, consciously or subconsciously. Dr. Cherry, meanwhile, is basking in her naivete, thinking Ash is as simple as she is. Releasing Ash isn't just unprofessional, it's unethical. The boy, the man, is dangerous. I want my objections on file because I'll accept no responsibility for it. And if you want to coast gently into retirement, Henry, neither should you."

Dr. Larkin paused, waiting for an agreement that never came.

"Speaking of careers, Ronald, there's something else we need to discuss." He held out papers for Dr. Larkin to take. "This is a Dr. Cherry's complaint of sexual harassment. The other copy's for your lawyer."

"*What?*"

"She alleges that on three separate occasions, you made 'lewd and demeaning comments to male colleagues regarding her last name. These alleged comments, and laughter, were well within her earshot."

And confirmed by all color rushing from Dr. Larkin's face.

"That was humor," Dr. Larkin responded, almost a whisper. "A few jokes. You have to understand—"

"I don't, though," Dr. Granville said, "and neither does she. What I'm pointing out is that your objections to Dr. Cherry's diagnosis today will be on record the same day she filed her complaint. You might want to consider how the timing of that will affect the Board of Review."

Near six o'clock, after Dr. Larkin had left his office, Dr. Granville remembered to once more look out his window. The red maple, glowing by the sunset behind it, seemed sparer already. Dead and dying leaves covered the grass below.

For a moment, it saddened him. But Henry Granville was a practical man. It was why he'd been hired to administer Bunyon Hospital in the first place. After winter, thin stalks on the tree's branches would sprout again, growing to the three tipped green leaves that would glow red again next fall.

In a week, he would lose one patient. But he knew without a doubt another would replace him, the result of nature no less expected than the tree's changing.

For better or for worse, Bunyon Psychiatric would remain at capacity.

CHAPTER 2

DR. CHERRY STOOD WITH MICHAEL ASH ON THE hospital's front lawn, waiting for the ride that would take him to his new life. A single suitcase in hand, wearing a white button-down shirt, black jeans, and sneakers, Michael stared through the hospital's iron fencing to the busy road beyond it. To Dr. Cherry, Michael looked as anxious as she was.

Her day had started with a visit to Michael's room to collect him. She knocked on his closed door. Closed doors were a privilege. It was good for Michael to experience privacy, if not yet locks.

No answer. Dr. Cherry knocked again, then turned the knob, pushing the solid wooden door open a few inches.

"Michael?"

No sound. No movement. Dr. Cherry felt discomfort, then dread. Where was he? Was her faith in Michael proving wrong even before his release?

She swung the door wide open. The room was empty. A suitcase sat on his crisply made bed, his window opened far enough for breezes to blow through iron bars beyond, catching his curtains. But where was Michael?

Stop. Breathe.

She looked down the hallway past patients and attendants to the group bathroom and shower facilities halfway down the corridor. Maybe Michael was there, running late but safe? Maybe he was still on the floor taking a final stroll? Maybe—

"Doctor?"

Startled, she looked back into the room. There he was, standing against the clean white wall beside the breeze-blown curtains. How did she miss him?

She let out her breath. Michael looked just as shaken, then relieved, as she was. They smiled at each other as he picked up his backpack and left the room.

Walking down the corridor, the number of patients who came to their doorways to watch Michael take his leave struck Dr. Cherry. They stared at him while he stared straight ahead. There were no 'goodbyes' or even questions about his leaving. Envy, she thought.

"Michael Ash!"

She and Michael stopped at the door of the center's poorly equipped library.

Mrs. Adler, a part-time volunteer and librarian, rushed toward them, her finger pointing at Michael.

"Where are my books?"

Michael stared back at her.

"I'm sorry, Mrs. Adler? What books?" Dr. Cherry asked.

"Borrowed books, or, at this late date, stolen ones," Mrs. Adler said.

Both women turned to him. "Michael?" asked Dr. Cherry.

"In my room?" Michael answered.

Dr. Cherry interrupted Mrs. Adler's demands for Michael to get them by promising to return them herself. The only thing that mattered now was getting Michael out of the building and on his way. She and Michael resumed their walk down the corridor at a faster pace. The lobby was now in sight when they saw Dr. Larkin waiting for them with what passed for a smile. Dammit, Dr. Cherry thought. She had successfully avoided him for the past week, hoping her luck would last.

"I'm so glad I caught you both," Dr. Larkin announced.

He's the only person, Dr. Cherry thought, who could make the word "glad" sound grimmer than "caught." Dr. Larkin waited for them in the center of the foyer, just far enough away from the security guards that their conversation wouldn't carry.

"I just got off the phone with David Chiba, the Administrator of the Tower Street Home. We had a long conversation about you, Mr. Ash. May I walk you out?"

Dr. Larkin opened the glass front doors for them to pass through. Dr. Cherry realized he had timed his appearance perfectly.

"Mr. Chiba was very grateful that I called. He even asked if I could visit sometime this week to address his staff. I told him I'd be delighted."

Descending the marble steps, they paused at the circular driveway leading to the hospital's gates.

"So, Mr. Ash, we will meet again soon."

Dr. Cherry saw the glint of anticipation in Dr. Larkin's eyes as obvious as the involuntary twitch of his lips. She looked at Michael and saw only the same keenness.

"So, you're aware, Dr. Cherry, I met with my lawyer to discuss our dispute. If your charge of sexual harassment reaches the Board, we will present a counterclaim of discrimination against the handicapped."

Taken aback, Dr. Cherry needed a moment to realize what Larkin was referring to. "You're not serious. That's outrageous!" she protested.

"So were your comments about my facial tics. My attorney also suggested I sign a statement summarizing our disagreements about Mr. Ash's release. That way, should there be repercussions, my opposition will be documented. My lawyer used the term 'criminal culpability.' Sparing the legalese, it makes certain that your head, not mine, will be on the prosecutor's platter."

Bidding them farewell, Dr. Cherry was certain Dr. Larkin had to restrain himself from skipping back to his office.

"We've made his day, Michael," Dr. Cherry said, watching Dr. Larkin. "Don't listen to him. He's a sad old man who shouldn't be treating people anymore."

"He treats you badly," Michael stated, watching Dr. Larkin's retreat. "He's a bad person."

"He is who he is. At his age, people don't change. There's nothing you can do about it."

She looked at Michael, who looked back at her and said nothing. Did he agree or disagree? He wasn't sure. Neither was she.

Michael squeezed her hand when the driver from the Tower Street Home arrived, or she squeezed his. The heavy metal playing from the van's radio reached them before the van did.

"Mike Ash? Scotty Schuster. No 'Scotty, beam me up,' okay? I hate Star Trek, but Avengers rule! Ready to rock?" The golden stud through the red-haired, eighteen-year-old's tongue didn't impede his speech or energy.

Michael frowned. "Something is stabbing your tongue."

"A tongue stud, man. You never saw a tongue stud before?"

"No, Scotty. Why aren't you bleeding?"

There's so much you haven't seen, Dr. Cherry thought. She helped Michael put on his backpack, heavier than she would have guessed. As she did, all the misgivings she'd suppressed overwhelmed her.

"You have my number, Michael. You know you can call me anytime, day or night."

"Day or night," he repeated.

"And I'll see you this week, okay? I can't wait to see your new home."

She hugged Michael hard and felt his tight embrace. "This will be great for you."

"Hey, Mike, you know what tonight is?" Scotty asked. "Taco Night! Load your own!"

Michael climbed into the front seat, looking back at Dr. Cherry. Scotty called goodbye, putting the van into gear. The van's automatic door locks clicked into place.

"Stop!" Michael shouted. Startled, Scott jammed on the brakes. "Buckle your seat belt. It's the law."

A beat. Then Scotty laughed. Michael joined him. Relieved, Dr. Cherry did, too.

———

MICHAEL SAT SILENTLY, staring out the car window at this world they hurtled through, a world that looked to exist to sell fast food. Michael had never been in any of these structures, but he remembered names from watching television at the hospital. He hummed under his breath.

Scotty, relishing his captive audience, told him his history, beginning with his battles with drugs and culminating with the unsympathetic court system. Michael listened at first, then began singing. The jingle for McDonald's led to a medley of tunes from many commercials he remembered.

Pulling onto the ramp of Route 71, Scotty was too annoyed at Michael's interruption to be concerned about the truck and trailer he cut off. Its driver, Bobby Lakes, laid on his horn. A large man who had already hauled furniture for nineteen nonstop hours from Kentucky, Lakes had even less goodwill

than he'd had sleep. He muttered a run of swearwords punctu-
ated by more honks.

"Kentucky," Scott noted from Lakes' license plate. "Probably rushing home to marry his sister."

Scott rolled down his window and shot Bobby Lakes the
finger, continuing his recital of the incompetence of court-
appointed lawyers. Following Scott's lead, Michael extended
his finger as well. Unlike Scott, he didn't retract it.

The truck's driver, angered at the doubled insult, followed
for one, two, then three miles before both vehicles braked to
stop for a light at an intersection. Putting his truck in park and
applying the safety brake, the bearded, nearly three-hundred-
pound driver jumped down from his rig, strode to the van, and
hammered at Scotty's window.

Michael withdrew his finger and looked over, curious.

"How 'bout you double assholes come on out and I'll break
off those fingers!"

"Chill, man," Scott replied. "Go back to Bumfuck."

"Get out here and say that!" Bobby shouted, kicking in the
metal panel of the van's door. "Do it now, Orphan Annie!"

The bright red of Scott's hair had always been a sensitive
topic to him. Not realizing Bobby's bulk because of the height
of his driver's seat, Scott threw open his door and climbed out.

Hearing a click to his right, Michael saw his door lock had
popped open as well.

Staring up at Bobby's flushed face a foot above his own,
Scotty realized he had made a serious mistake. As Bobby
grabbed him by the shirtfront, flashbacks of several playground
beatings filled his head.

"I'm sorry, man," Scotty told the angry giant, "I swear! I
was just fuckin' with you."

"Watch me fucking rip that earring off your tongue!"

Hearing Bobby Lake speak, Michael instinctively recognized who he was. He had seen men just like him on the hospital's TV. Bad men, in a movie he had seen twice because he liked listening to the skinny, backwoods boy who played banjo.

"Let him go, weasel dick, or I'll kick your cracker ass!" Michael called.

Scotty looked in surprise at Michael standing a few feet away, his eyes locked with Bobby's.

"You think I can't kick both your asses?"

"You want to squeal like a pig and get me all excited?"

Scott felt panic growing as Michael strode to the massive truck driver. Why is he doing this? Is he suicidal? And what the hell is this instant Southern accent?

The light changed. Here on the highway, with the Brook Meadow Mall to their right, traffic was heavy and constant. Cars far behind them honked their horns while nearer motorists rolled down their windows to hear the fight they eagerly awaited.

Michael stopped before Bobby. "Now let him go. You got 'till three. You need help counting, Goober? One."

Bobby stared into the eyes of the smaller man. He couldn't say how, but he recognized his own hair-trigger temper. And something else, something puzzling, that he didn't recognize.

"You are one crazy sonofabitch," Bobby determined.

"And you are the other one," Michael said.

Scott stood amazed as Bobby Lakes, then Michael, broke into laughter, shaking hands and punching each other's arms while swapping insults involving their parents' sex lives. Cars behind them honked longer as those beside them drove off in disappointment.

Bobby was on his way back to his truck, still laughing, when Scotty urged Michael, standing on the highway's double white line, "Now let's get the hell out of here."

Michael didn't move, even with cars speeding past him.

"Now! Let's go!" Scott urged.

"Go where?" Michael asked indifferently, his voice drawl free.

"Home!" Scott replied.

Michael nodded. After over twenty years, he couldn't be readier. He *was* going home as soon as he found out where that was. To find home, he had to find his brother. Home was wherever Justin was.

"I'm going," Michael said. He turned away, shifting his backpack, then stepping into traffic that skidded to a stop before him.

"Michael!" Scotty called over more horn blasts and squeals of brakes. "Come on, man! Get back here."

Michael reached the other side of the highway before looking back.

"Thank you for the ride, Scotty," he called over the traffic lanes. "I don't like tacos."

About to follow him, Scotty stepped back as a trailer truck rushed past within inches. When it cleared him, Michael was gone.

Confused, Scotty climbed back into the Tower Street van. He reached for his cell phone to call ahead, but the shouts of angry drivers behind him changed his mind.

Scotty put the van in gear. He'd tell Mr. Chiba what happened when he was safely parked in their driveway. Not his fault, Scotty told himself. I'm a driver, not a counselor, not a babysitter. It's all good. More tacos for me.

CHAPTER 3

Dr. Larkin pulled into the driveway of his ranch house at half-past eight, belching more of the Broiled Fisherman's Platter he had methodically worked through at a local chain restaurant.

More disturbing than the mediocre meal was nearly missing the Early Bird Special. Before reaching sixty-five, Dr. Larkin had been insulted whenever a waiter asked if he qualified for Golden Age discounts. Now, reaching it, economics triumphed over pride.

Tonight, he had argued with the manager loudly enough for all the dining room to hear that their clock was fast, insisting that he walked in the door ten minutes before, not after six. Worn down, the manager agreed, then debated all the way to the kitchen which secret ingredients he'd add to Dr. Larkin's meal.

Dr. Larkin watched the garage door rise, revealing his spotless parking spot and workspace, its whitewashed concrete floor swept clean. In the rear of the garage was his workshop bench. Each tool hung in its proper place, indicated by a painted red silhouette of the tool itself. Suspended from the ceiling were a half dozen buckets, all clearly labeled from "Rock Salt" to "Sawdust" with the help of his label maker.

His ex-wife, Florence, had shaken her head, seeing the endless labels for the last time as she climbed into her car to leave him.

"I'm surprised you can still breathe, Ronald," were her last words. "I don't see a bucket labeled *air*."

He took his briefcase from the back seat containing Michael Ash's records. True, he was violating hospital policy by removing them from the premises and, yes, breaching patient confidentiality by copying them for his lawyer, but neither act bothered him. He was sworn to self-preservation long before he swore the Hippocratic Oath.

The red outlines of his absent bow saw and claw hammer caught his eye.

Did he leave the saw in the yard when he was trimming branches off his pear tree? Possibly. But where's the hammer? Did he lend it to a neighbor? No, of course not. He never lent anyone a tool in his life. Scolding himself for slackness, he unlocked the door leading to the house, which was similarly organized: everything, and everyone, in their place.

Entering the kitchen, he put down his briefcase and opened the "Miscellaneous" drawer for toothpicks. Dr. Larkin frowned. The toothpick box normally sitting beside his twine, tape, and scissors was missing. He looked at the "To Get" list on the side of his refrigerator. Mustard and sardines were listed, but no toothpicks. His system had failed. Dr. Larkin wrote "toothpicks" on the "To Get" list. With his tongue, he worked at dislodging a shrimp skin caught between two bottom teeth. Stubbornly, it remained. Today, nothing would be easy.

Dr. Larkin entered his bathroom, took his toothbrush, and brushed fiercely enough for his gums to bleed. Still, the shrimp hung in. The only thing shaken loose was his hair. He pulled off his toupee so it wouldn't fall into the wet sink and put it on the hamper top, out of harm's way. Quickly washing his hands, he reached into his mouth and pulled out his dentures, spotting the offending shrimp immediately.

Holding his teeth, Dr. Larkin attacked them again with his brush, rinsed, and searched for shrimp. Nothing left. Perfect.

Dr. Larkin opened his mouth to return his teeth, raising his head to stare in the mirror, and saw him. Michael Ash stared back. The doctor's teeth clinked as he released them into the porcelain washbowl.

Michael recognized his fear. He studied Dr. Larkin's emotion in the same way he had studied twenty years of dread and horror on television.

"You lied to me," Michael stated.

Before he could deny a thing, the doctor watched Michael hold up the patient file he had taken from Larkin's briefcase.

"You said you didn't know where my brother is," Michael stated.

"I never said that, exactly."

"You just lied again." Michael held up Dr. Larkin's wig with one hand. "You lie a lot."

Carefully, Michael put down his file on the bed, picking up the claw hammer he had placed there.

"Michael, put that down." Dr. Larkin listened to the sound of his voice and the panic in it.

Michael tilted his head. "Doctor," he said, "you are not a good person."

Taking a deep breath, Dr. Larkin slowly moved closer. "Michael, we can negotiate this. All you need to do is hand me the hammer. Give it to me. Now."

And Michael did.

CHAPTER 4

Dr. Maureen Cherry's phone rang, exploding her sleep. Scooping the phone from its base on the bedstand, she glanced at her fluorescent alarm clock. Call it late night or early morning, the hour was ungodly.

"Hello?"

She swung her legs off the bed, suddenly wide awake and rapt.

"I've no idea," she answered, "I haven't seen him since you picked him up... No, I don't mean you, I mean your driver... yes. But how could Michael just walk away and disappear? How long have you looked? Have you called the police?"

Maureen hoped they had, hoped the police had notified Dr. Granville as well, but she heard only more bad news. Since she was listed as Michael's contact, they had called her first. Asking the administrator of the Tower Street Home to call back with any information, she put down the phone and assessed her priorities. She would call Dr. Granville first, go out to search for Michael herself, and then, only when he was safely back at Bunyon Psychiatric, begin her job hunt for any employment she could find within a few hours' drive.

Reaching to turn on her bedside lamp, she realized the

room was already dimly lit. Glowing through the blinds on her window was the yellow back porch light she must have left on.

Maureen pulled on her robe and walked down the carpeted hallway, stopping to look in on her eleven-year-old daughter, Anna, turning in bed. On a wall poster, a singer glared accusingly through her mascara. One more pre-teen "role model" she loathed silently. She had long realized that any negative comments she was foolish enough to make would raise the singer's status from pop tart to icon.

She stopped on the last stair, the kitchen before her.

Something was wrong. The porch light illuminated the small table and chairs, the counters and closed cabinets. But still—

CRASH.

It was the door. Closed, yes, but through its top three window panels she could see the storm door behind it was ajar. The wind caught it, whipping it open, only to bang it back.

The slam startled her. She hesitated before walking toward it. She had locked her back door. She was sure of it. So, if it was still locked, everything was all right. She forced herself to take one step toward it, then another, her hand reaching for the door handle—

"Mom?"

Maureen jumped, knowing even as she did it was her daughter's voice.

Anna stood halfway down the carpeted steps, still half asleep until jolted by her mother's panic.

"What?" Anna demanded, now anxious.

"What's wrong?"

"Nothing is wrong."

"The phone rang."

"It was a work call. I have to go in early. I'm going to call your father. I'll stay until he gets here. He'll be happy to have you for a long weekend."

Anna knew her mother was hiding something. She could continue her questions or she could go back to bed.

"Okay."

Dr. Cherry waited until she heard Anna climb the stairs and flop back onto her mattress before turning back to the door and testing its handle.

Locked.

Rattling it, relief swept through her when it wouldn't budge. Still holding the handle, she remembered the call yet to be made to Dr. Granville. She could delay it another minute.

Maureen pushed up on her toes to look through the middle of the round glass panel. She saw nothing but the back porch, a small cement block with two steps down to the communal yard beyond it, also empty. A pen for garbage cans a hundred feet away.

For the first time, she was grateful the Townhouse Property Committee hadn't yet agreed on a landscaper. Patches of grass now and nothing else. Not a tree, a bush, nothing anyone could hide behind.

The storm door swung back and forth from the night's breezes. She unlocked the back door, pulled it toward her, then screamed, leaping back instinctively. She collided with a kitchen chair and drove it backward, scraping over the floor until they both crashed into the wall and could go no farther.

Even then, she tried to escape, her bare feet shooting out from beneath her as she fell to the floor. And then it was worse. She was level with it.

Anna shouted for her. She heard her footsteps. She shouted for Anna to stay upstairs, as she stared at the blood-wet object she finally recognized.

In the doorway, centered on an elegant silver platter, rested the head of Dr. Ronald Larkin. Eyes and mouth open, it stared back at her, its expression equally horrified.

A toothpick pinned a paper through the wig into the tongue dripping with crimson. A page from a prescription pad.

She couldn't stop herself. She had to look at the message. She pulled the paper off the toothpick, looked back at the head in disbelief, then read the note.

"Doctor Cherry, yours is safe now. Michael."

CHAPTER 5

Owen Moser stood in his underpants, glaring at the policeman.

It would be hard to say which of them was more repulsed: the young sergeant, who pounded on Moser's rented Sarasota condo door loudly enough for two neighbors to appear, or Moser himself, outraged to be woken before noon to face a cop and a hangover.

"*Detective* Owen Moser?"

"Uh-huh."

"You don't have a phone?"

"If I did, I'd get phone calls."

The sergeant looked past Moser to see a mound of magazines and food delivery boxes spilled out over the carpet. Enough talk, he decided. Moser wasn't worth his time.

"We got this call at the precinct." He handed the message sheet to Moser. "They say it's urgent."

"Uh-huh."

The sergeant waited. Moser didn't even glance at the paper. "You want a tip?"

"No, but I've got one for you. If you get behind a wheel

before you sober up, I will lock up your drunk ass with great joy, no matter who you are."

Moser considered this. "Fair enough," he said. He crumpled up the message, tossing it over his shoulder before closing the door in the sergeant's face.

After three more hours of sleep, Moser returned to the living room, reluctantly lifting a blind slat just enough to see. Sun. Always sun. One more thing to hate about Florida.

He saw the discarded message on the carpet and stepped over it into the kitchen.

Determined to ignore the nearly emptied Chivas bottle on the counter, he opened the refrigerator and pulled out a Coors Light. Two birds with one stone, Moser reasoned as he popped the tab: a hangover helper and, having run out of toothpaste, a mouthwash bound to kill as many bacteria as brain cells.

Finishing the beer, Moser returned to the living room, turning on a lamp rather than opening the blinds. He stared at the balled-up paper, weighing the pros and cons of picking it up. Useless energy expended if the message was just one more from his former precinct or union rep. Who else could it be from? His partner, Steve Hayden, gave up trying to contact him after four months and twice that many letters.

But for the paper to be laying there on the carpet... that was annoying. Unlike trash, he couldn't leave it there with the scrawled message in view. How many times, day and night, would he have to walk past the message to become irritated all over again?

Could he learn to ignore it? Not likely. It was one thing Moser knew all too well about himself. When it came to forgetting, he couldn't.

He took a step closer, unable to decipher the wrinkled paper from this height. There was also the alternative, he realized, of picking it up and pitching it into the trash without another glance.

Sighing, Moser bent over, feeling waves of blood crash to his temples.

He'd decide whether to read it on his way up.

————

THIRTY MINUTES LATER, his phone recharged, Moser paced the pier and listened.

"You are a selfish, miserable, son of a bitch who is no longer my friend."

"You tracked me down to say that, Steve?"

"Just so you know, this is all about the job."

"The job. Got it."

"You remember Michael Ash from Bunyon Psychiatric?"

Suddenly, Moser felt all too sober, more painfully clear-headed than he had in months. "Yeah," he answered, "I remember."

"They let him out three days ago."

"Why?"

"Because some stupid shrink said he wasn't dangerous and nobody told her he was still crazy." Hayden paused, knowing what was coming would hurt. "And that includes you, Owen."

Moser looked across the waters of the Sarasota Marina, feeling a chill in the eighty-degree breezes.

"Nobody called me."

"You have no phone. Dr. Cherry says she wrote asking for your input. When there was no response, they pushed Ash out the door."

Moser closed his eyes, his headache fiercer than the one he got off the plane with at Sarasota Airport over six months ago.

"Owen?"

"What happened?"

"Ash got out of a van taking him to a halfway house. Same night, he kills one of Bunyon's shrinks, then disappears, after leaving the guy's head on a platter at Cherry's back door. That was last night."

"And now?"

"He's gone with the fucking wind."

"He had a brother. The brother got adopted."

"Your files told us that much. But that's another dead end. We can't find him."

"There've got to be records."

"There are. First-class, computerized records going back twenty years. The kid was adopted twenty-two years ago. Those files haven't been inputted yet."

"So they're on paper somewhere."

"Not anymore. There was a fire five years ago at the warehouse repository for the adoption records."

"Okay. What about patient files from the hospital?"

"Plenty of them. All except the one for Michael Ash. So, Owen, what can you tell me?"

Moser turned over the question in his mind. What *should* he tell him?

"You saw Ash, what, a year ago when we investigated the jumper's suicide at the hospital?"

"Right."

"You talked to him."

"You know I did."

A silence, uncomfortable for both of them.

"Owen, just tell me this. Did he say anything, anything at all, that could help us now?"

"No."

"Are you sure?" There was more relief than frustration in Hayden's voice. "Tell me if you're not. You're not on trial here."

How wrong you are, Moser thought. I've been on trial for six months and eleven days. And now a second crime, just as horrific, had been added to his charges against himself. But Moser could suffer for them both. Alone. He didn't need Hayden to share the responsibility.

"You couldn't have stopped this, Steve. Ash was mine. It was my call."

Now it was his partner's turn to hesitate. "Owen, listen to me. I can go to the Chief for you. He knows what you've gone through. I think he'd let a lot of things slide."

"Which things? That it's my twenty-fifth week of a two-week leave, or that I write 'Occupant Deceased' on every letter he sent me?"

"But—"

"Steve, like it or not, I'm still your friend. But I'm going to hang up now."

Moser ended the call and looked out at the dozen yachts anchored off the dock, any of them costing more than every combined paycheck he had ever cashed. Not a soul in sight on a single boat. Where were the owners? In tall buildings, making more money to play with, or watching their bank accounts breed rather than staring at the sunset?

How hard would it be to hotwire one ignition and sail out of the marina onto the ocean, searching for that point the ancients feared: the end of the earth, the drop into nothingness?

BACK AT HIS CONDO, it took Moser only minutes to pack, moving faster than he had in months. Tickets? He'd get them at the airport. The ride there? He'd call an Uber. Who most deserved to be behind bars, Michael Ash or himself? That he had no answer for.

On the way out of the bedroom, Moser stopped, picking up the framed photograph on the bamboo dresser. Their wedding picture. Peggy and him on the dance floor. She was beautiful. He had hair. It began its retreat soon after, but Peggy always kept her beauty. It grew greater every day he knew her. Even at the end, she was still the most beautiful woman he'd ever known. That had never changed, even when all else did.

He looked at the photograph, seeing her face filled with joy, for that moment and their future.

Gently, Moser placed the picture back on the dresser, face down. He would never want Peggy to see him this way.

CHAPTER 6

Why would anyone stop for strangers?

He wouldn't. It was not intelligent. But they did stop, trucks and cars and vans, almost all driven by men. And though Michael disapproved, he still understood all who pulled over to pick him up, those who needed to talk, and those who nursed their silence.

Michael knew each driver by their posture, their grip on the wheel, the lines in their faces. He knew them through or despite the words they spoke and the tones they spoke them with.

One Cadillac driver, a "regional distributor" with an American flag tie hanging from his neck, filled silences with non-stop stories, punchlines called out as challenges to meet with equal volumes of laughter.

Michael whooped and hooted, grinned and chuckled. He slapped his leg or held his belly in the protective way the driver did. Michael even told a joke, making it up as he went along. Hollering its conclusion, he was rewarded with echoes of laughter, even though it made no sense at all.

The distributor seemed sad to drop him off, and Michael

knew why. He was the Perfect Passenger, providing each driver with their ideal audience: themself.

The young Russian driver was hesitant to try out his textbook English until his hitchhiker with a speech impediment seemed even more self-conscious. The white-haired driver returning from the funeral of his boyhood friend, eager to talk about an afterlife, was grateful for the spiritual assurances his passenger provided.

Only one ride made Michael uneasy.

———

MARYLAND, 295 North.

A gleaming green convertible swung off the highway, braking to a stop a bare dozen feet before him. Even as Michael took his seat inside the sports car, he sensed the driver's nervousness, but it was too late. The vehicle had already pulled back into traffic.

Michael stared at the driver, who looked barely old enough to be in high school. The boy blushed, feeling Michael's eyes upon him.

"I just got it. The car. It's my birthday present."

Michael considered the tone of his voice. Boastful, but defensive.

"It's nice," he offered.

The boy laughed. "A Jaguar X KR? Yeah!"

"I like the color," Michael tried again. "The green."

"Olive," the young man corrected him.

A car horn honked.

Michael turned to see two girls in a van in the middle lane, keeping pace with the gleaming convertible. The freckled, red-haired driver shouted words Michael couldn't hear while both girls waved and smiled.

"Ignore them," Michael's driver pleaded.

"All right."

The boy stepped lightly on the gas pedal and the girls' van fell far behind them.

"This thing can go from 0 to 60 in 5.3 seconds," he said, almost apologetically.

"Why?" Michael asked.

"Exactly. I told my dad if he insisted on buying me a car, all I wanted was a jeep or an SUV."

"SUV?" Michael thought he remembered seeing a TV show with initials.

"Right. Nothing that stood out. But my dad's dad bought him a Jag when he was seventeen. It's a family tradition. So now I can't trust any girl I meet, because, to her, I'm like a car accessory. They're turned on by my Jag or my money."

Michael thought about this, unsure if he should smile at what might be irony, or nod to indicate empathy for the driver's rueful confession.

"What's your name?" he asked, instead.

"Gordon. Yours?"

"Michael," he answered. He sensed Gordon relaxing. Maybe it was better to continue in this manner, to speak about himself rather than Gordon or his car. He volunteered a simple fact about himself.

"I have no money," Michael shared.

"No?" Gordon looked at Michael, uncertain where this was going.

"They gave me twenty dollars when I left the hospital, but I used it yesterday to eat." Michael knew he said something wrong from the tension returning to Gordon's face.

They passed a highway sign filled with logos for fast food and gasoline.

"I'm going to pull over at this rest stop," Gordon said. "You can get something to eat there."

His voice was higher now, his eyes wider. Michael absorbed his stress. He disliked feeling this way.

"I'm not hungry," Michael said. "And I told you, I don't have any money."

"Don't worry about that," Gordon insisted.

He's afraid, Michael realized. Everything he'd said was wrong. Staring at Gordon, Michael spotted something colorful in his peripheral vision. He reached into the back seat and picked it up for a closer look: a metal bar with two solid hooks, part of it covered in orange rubber.

"What's this?" Michael asked.

"The Club. A friend gave it to me as a joke." Gordon paused. "This car already has theft protection. Great protection. The police can track where it goes. Anywhere. I'm pulling off, now."

"The Club." Michael saw its name printed on the rubber handle. He tested its weight, hitting his left hand with the club in his right. Three, maybe four pounds. Gordon accelerated slightly with every blow.

Michael wondered if a whack with this club would deter any car thief.

"I don't think this can protect you," he told Gordon.

They sped off the exit ramp, passing the gas station, and stopping directly in front of the building housing the food bazaar.

Gordon turned to Michael as he took out his wallet. "Here. Take this."

He pulled from it a thick handful of bills. Surprised, Michael looked from him to the money in his hand. He tried to understand Gordon's anxiety, but now his own made logic impossible.

"Please, get out," Gordon begged.

Other travelers rolled by, checking out the car, but Michael felt on display. He quickly climbed from the Jaguar.

"Gordon?" Michael looked in through the passenger window.

"What?"

"Happy Birthday."

Gordon left black rubber tracks behind in his haste to get back on the highway. It couldn't be good for the tires, Michael thought.

A mustached man wearing a "Great Adventure" cap stood next to Michael, watching the Jaguar speed away. "Crazy," he said.

Michael didn't like that word but felt this time it might be warranted. In the clump of bills Gordon had pushed at him, he spotted a credit card as well.

"Crazy," Michael agreed.

————

HE WAS HUNGRY NOW. He went into the building, stopping in the middle of the food court.

Michael swung in a half-circle, paralyzed by too many choices. A little red-haired girl's hamburgers, a goateed colonel's chicken, and, unaccountably, sandwiches from a subway between them. He had more than enough money now to try them all. And would.

After eating himself full, Michael reached into the back-pack beside him. It was difficult to pull the book he wanted free from all the others overstuffed into the canvas bag.

My Body was a biology textbook from Bunyon Hospital's library targeted at high school students. Habitually, Michael opened it to the middle, to what he once called at twelve years old the "cartoons."

A fully naked man was painted head to toe on the plastic sheet. Brightly colored, the illustration was an oasis for the eye in the otherwise black and white volume.

Michael quickly flipped that page. He had no interest in the man's outward appearance, in skin everyone in the world could see. His interest was in the treasures beneath it, the network of organs that gave life, or, if failing, took that life and their own.

He paged through the transparencies, revealing the body's interior as if sliced into horizontal levels. Skeletal system, respiratory system. Here, the neck. Dr. Larkin's neck. Michael stared and remembered.

Standing behind him with the hammer, he had swung it to connect with the side of Dr. Larkin's head just behind his temple. The weakest part of the skull, the pterion region, where the frontal, parietal, temporal, and sphenoid bones met.

Dr. Larkin had dropped to the floor as if every bone in his body was broken.

The bow saw was brand new, Michael had noted as he ran it across the doctor's neck.

Scrutinizing the book's illustration, Michael compared it to the memory of what he saw as he severed the head. He had estimated correctly, making his incision between the second and third vertebrae. There, the trachea, a narrower passageway than it looked from the book's image. Higher, the larynx, the voice box. The clavicle and spinal cord took more pressure to split apart. Michael's attention was split between his anatomy lesson and his study of Dr. Larkin's last eleven seconds of life. Despite the blow to his head, the doctor's closed eyes popped open at the saw's first gash. As his eyelids fluttered, his lips contracted. His mouth opened for a soundless scream. Eyelids shut, lips compressed, and then the eyes opened again, even wider this time. Dr. Larkin's pupils seemed to fasten onto his. Michael wondered if he recognized him, and hoped so. Over the last four seconds, the doctor's eyes glazed over as if he was staring within himself.

Michael closed the book, surprised to find himself not fully satisfied. Why? He had touched a life and watched as it left his hands.

His vocal cords. He didn't see Dr. Larkin's vocal cords. He hadn't studied them, imagined how they'd create the doctor's reedy, unpleasant tones. He should have removed his voice box, held it in his hands. A missed opportunity.

Michael put his arms through his backpack and walked toward the doors to the parking lot, where he would find another ride.

Remember this next time, he noted. Take time to explore.

CHAPTER 7

This is payback, Moser thought.

It had been far too easy to show his suspended badge and I.D. to gain entry to Bunyon Psychiatric Hospital and even easier to find Dr. Cherry, who agreed to speak with him immediately.

But now, taking a seat in her office, Moser wanted a drink and a cigarette just as much as he wanted answers. He forced himself to focus on Dr. Cherry's explanation of the history of Michael Ash's treatment at Bunyon Psychiatric.

"Doctor," he interrupted, "could you explain this to me like you're on FOX, not NPR?"

She nodded eagerly. "Dr. Larkin believed Michael was caught in the mid-phase of a narcissistic personality disorder, that he never moved past the stage of 'Mirror Transference.' But in Michael's case—"

"Back up."

Dr. Cherry thought for a moment. "You're the policeman who arrested Michael when he was a little boy?"

"I brought him in. He was eight. His prints were all over the baseball bat. His brother Justin, who was five, could barely lift it. Michael admitted to killing his parents. He never changed his story. There's no doubt he did it."

"I wasn't trying to suggest there was. That was before my time here. Michael's medical records and court transcripts both made it clear he was an abused child—"

"I know that."

"What I'm saying is that this all ties together. A patient often looks at their therapist as a parental figure, and with Michael's background, that kind of relationship would be much more complicated. The psychiatrist Heinz Kohut wrote about what he called Transference Response, the tendency for a person in analysis to 'transfer' particulars of his personality onto his analyst. It's a positive step, really. It can precede a patient moving toward his own ego's equilibrium, toward a cure. By being able to project his personality onto a second party, the patient can see aspects of their own identity more clearly. Kohut described several types of these configurations, one of them being 'Mirror Transference.' But with Michael, it was the complete opposite. Dr. Larkin thought he was less self-reflective than reflective of whoever he was with. That it was Michael holding the mirror, not staring into it. Does that make sense?"

All too much sense. Moser shifted uncomfortably in his seat, which Dr. Cherry interpreted as confusion.

"Maybe I can explain it this way: at your station, don't you have two-way mirrors at your police station? A room with a mirror that when the criminal looks at it he sees himself, but on the other side you can look straight through it and see the criminal?"

Moser nodded. She watches TV. "Go on."

"Dr. Larkin believed that Michael's worldview was based on a variation of the two-way mirror. Michael sat where you are, looking through the mirror at me, and saw... no, somehow *sensed* the dynamics of my personality. So, when I looked back—"

"You saw yourself."

"Exactly. Because Michael *became* the mirror. He showed you the person you'd most likely relate to: yourself. With his upbringing of abuse, it would be the perfect way for Michael to protect himself. It sounds farfetched."

"Not really," Moser thought out loud. "When I was a little kid, I remember sitting at the kitchen table listening to my mother when she'd talk on the phone with her friends."

Dr. Cherry waited for him to go on.

"After she'd say 'hello,' I'd hear her voice change. Not a lot, but a little. Enough to know who she was talking to."

"How do you mean?"

"Well, if she was talking to Mrs. Micci, her voice would be lighter, happier, more like Mrs. Micci's personality. But if she was talking with Mrs. La Pierre, her voice sounded a lot more serious. When she'd get off the phone, I'd say to her, 'You were talking to so and so,' and she'd always be surprised I knew."

"It's a common behavior that we adapt to someone else's speech rhythms," Dr. Cherry agreed. "But Dr. Larkin wasn't just talking about empathy. He believed Michael was completely antisocial at his core, that he absorbed the characteristics of those around him for a deliberate reason, to use against them. I thought it was a faulty diagnosis myself, and I never gave it credence."

"Why not?"

"I think it's fair to say that Dr. Larkin had an extremely abrasive personality. When he dealt with Michael, Michael became equally abrasive. A very common interpersonal response."

"But when you treated him?"

Dr. Cherry hesitated. She'd been played, personally and professionally.

"I found Michael to be intelligent and empathetic. I was amazed to see such positive characteristics despite his abuse."

"Would you describe yourself as intelligent and empathetic?"

Dr. Cherry saw where Moser was going and tried to deflect. "You have to understand that all mental health professionals show a certain degree of empathy. Or so we hope. But there also needs to be a clinical distance. I certainly never opened myself enough to reveal personality traits Michael could have imprinted on."

"So, *you* were a perfect mirror."

"In that sense, yes."

Moser noted her rising defensiveness. She wouldn't be any help to him remaining that way.

"You seem easy enough to talk to. Open, receptive. That's a good thing for a doctor or anyone. You shouldn't feel any guilt for what happened. I'm sure Michael would find your personality a lot easier to live with than his own. If he has one."

"You're oversimplifying."

Or hitting a nerve, Moser thought.

"Mirror Transference isn't something that develops overnight," she maintained, "it's a stage of a patient's treatment where he needs to see his *own* qualities in someone else. It takes time for that to happen. So if you're implying that if I walked into a room and Michael instantly *became* me, that's completely impossible."

She paused.

"So as far as 'guilt'? The fact I didn't see the anger in him that caused him to kill Dr. Larkin? Of course I feel guilt. The frustration of not knowing if I could have made a difference. Just as I'm sure you feel."

"Me?"

"Yes. Because if you *had* felt it was unwise to release Michael, I'm sure you would have responded to the letter I sent you."

Touché, thought Moser.

"You're talking about a kid I met when he was eight years old."

Dr. Cherry frowned. "Didn't you meet him again? A year or two ago? I thought I read in his file you interviewed him after Benny Weill's suicide?"

Time to lie or leave, Moser thought. Catholic grammar school, then high school. You can leave the church, but the church never leaves you. "That's right. I saw him again."

"Then you tell me. You're a professional, you have instincts. Did you ever see Michael become at all violent?"

Say you didn't, her eyes pleaded.

Moser stood, ready to close the conversation. "I saw the results when he did," he replied.

"When you were on the force, that is."

Moser and Dr. Cherry looked to her office doorway, where Bunyon's administrator, Dr. Henry Granville, stood with his arms crossed.

"He is," Dr. Cherry said quickly, eager to avoid another misstep. "This is Detective Moser."

"That's what he told our receptionist," Granville said, looking at Moser. "We already had two detectives visit us early this morning. I just got off the phone with Detective Hayden, who told me Mr. Moser has no part in this investigation. He's officially on leave."

"Which I'm about to do," Moser said, forcing Granville to step back enough for him to pass. "You know what they say about retired detectives."

As Moser left them, Drs. Granville and Cherry wondered

what they say about old detectives. Moser had no clue, no punchline. To him, there were no retired detectives.

———

MOSER'S GETAWAY wasn't fast enough.

In the parking lot, as he backed up his car, Steve Hayden drove down the row directly behind him and stopped, blocking him in.

"Have you lost your mind?" Hayden shouted as he climbed from his Toyota. "You come back into town and don't even *call* the station? You're suspended, Owen! You're not a cop! What the hell were you doing in there?"

"You wanted to know more about Michael Ash."

"So you do me this big favor of slipping back into town and pretending nothing happened?"

"No," Moser cut him off, "plenty has happened. We both know that."

Hayden looked away, trying to let go of his anger. "Let's go back to the station. See the captain. Work things out."

Moser stopped him. "I'm not here, Jack. I'm still on leave. Move your car and I'm out of here."

Hayden noticed Moser's car for the first time.

"It's Peggy's," Moser confirmed. "Seventeen years old. Started right up for me."

Hayden nodded, remembering. Moser had bought the shining blue Miata convertible to surprise Peggy. Both men stared at the vanity plate she had insisted on, "OVRTIME."

"Practically need a crane to lower myself in," Moser added.

"It was a hell of a Christmas present," Hayden said. Neither man could help but smile.

"How's Grace?" Moser asked.

"Happy. She sold a lot of houses this year."

"Great. The kids?"

"Elizabeth's a junior. Ron's a freshman at Emerson. Full scholarship."

"Baseball?"

"No. Robotics. Maybe the video games weren't a total waste of time."

"Good for him. And you and Grace. Give them my love, okay?"

"Come for dinner tonight. Tell them yourself."

"I'll be on the road. Maybe next time."

He wouldn't, but neither man needed to say so. They shook hands, waited a moment for the other to lean in for a hug. Neither did. Hayden waited, watching Moser climb gingerly into the low-slung coupe, wedging himself behind the wheel as he exhaled.

"Owen."

Moser looked up at Hayden, now towering over him.

"You've got to come back to life. You're being a self-indulgent asshole, the kind of guy you always hated. You're not the first man who lost his wife."

"I know that," Moser said, "But I didn't lose her, Steve. I killed her."

Hayden stared at Moser, trying to think of anything to say that he hadn't before. When he couldn't, he got back into his car and moved it.

CHAPTER 8

**_BEDFORD VILLAGE, WESTCHESTER COUNTY, NEW YORK
State. October 27th._**

IT WASN'T until Michael was dropped off in front of the small
clapboard post office that he realized why the town seemed so
familiar.

An old-fashioned, tree-lined Main Street. A row of stores
and a movie theater. A library, delicatessen, and firehouse faced
the triangular village green framed by two beautiful churches,
Presbyterian and Catholic, one wood, one stone.

Picture perfect colonial buildings, bricks and boards
painted antique white. Picture perfect people on the street who
wouldn't think of passing someone else without a nod or
greeting.

There, Michael thought, scanning Main Street. There's the
library Donna Reed worked at as a lonely spinster. And at the
edge of the green, hundreds of years old, the tree Jimmy
Stewart crashed his car into during the Christmas Eve storm.

"*It's a Wonderful Life,*" Michael realized. Bedford Village
was Bedford Falls.

He had seen the movie countless times in the patient's lounge. It was one of those films the staff would hurry patients in to see, with the same firmness they'd insist on punctuality taking their meds. "It's good for you."

The TV was mounted in the corner of the room and attached to the ceiling so no one could change channels but the shift supervisors, who carried the power of the Remote Control with them at all times.

Looking at those watching the movie, Michael learned even by his second viewing where the adults laughed and where they brushed tears away with Kleenex. Reactions came from the most unlikely staff persons and patients, even the angriest, the most disassociated.

Two years ago, Michael remembered, even Benny Weill watched riveted. Benny, a guard at Bunyon, was a very bad man. Still, at the final scene of fellowship in the Bailey living room, Benny shouted at the patients around him to "shut up or else!"

Michael knew when he should smile or sigh, making him as inconspicuous as any other patient. As with all television shows or movies, Michael marveled at how easily viewers were drawn into them. Even knowing that the people and stories they were watching were simply lies, Bunyon's staff and patients eagerly welcomed them. Make-believe in black and white or color. A man and woman on screen pretending to be who they weren't in a world as imaginary as who they pretended to be. And there were so many.

A smiling sheriff takes a young boy fishing, deaf to the whistling that followed them. Michael never saw any policeman look happy.

A heavy man who never leaves his kitchen threatens to hit his wife so hard she'll land on the moon, causing bursts of laughter from the television and viewers in the patient's lounge simultaneously.

Their behavior was not intelligent. Michael had decided that long ago. But each action and reaction was a valuable opportunity for him to learn.

It's a Wonderful Life fascinated Michael in other ways than a behavioral study. Often, since he first saw the film at nine years old, he asked himself the same question the angel Clarence posed.

What if he, Michael Ash, had never been born?

Like George Bailey's brother Harry, Michael's brother Justin would have had a different life. Harry Bailey crashed through the pond's ice and would have drowned without George to rescue him. Imagine Justin's fate, alone in a life sure to be filled with harm and hatred, with no chance of escaping.

Then there was George Bailey's special gift to consider. A man who could walk through a world he knew, yet was unknown in, thanks to Clarence's powers. Michael enjoyed the idea of that very much: George Bailey's past becoming as invisible as the angel Clarence in his present.

Michael had learned to be nearly as invisible as far back as he could remember, with no one's assistance. He didn't need an angel.

On the community bulletin board standing on posts before the post office, Michael spotted a map of Bedford Village and its surrounding towns, Pound Ridge, Mt. Kisco, Chappaqua.

He studied it while an elderly lady, with hair so white it seemed to glow, passed and wished him a good morning. Michael returned her greeting, then turned back to the map to find the street where his brother lived.

What a wonderful place this must have been to grow up in.

He heard the bells hung on the post office's front door

jingle as the white-haired lady pushed it open. Michael smiled at their ringing.

'*Atta boy, Clarence,* Michael thought to himself. '*Atta boy.*

CHAPTER 9

"SISTER?" Moser asked, "Sister Dolorine? I'm here to ask about a boy you knew back in 1980. Do you remember Justin Ash?"

No reply. He looked at the ninety-six-year-old woman seated beside him in an Adirondack chair that needed painting. She stared straight ahead, not moving.

I've seen faces like hers carved on potatoes, Moser reflected. But even then, a dried-out potato couldn't match this woman's wrinkles. It was as if she had once been broken into a million pieces and then glued back together, every crack displayed proudly.

Moser tried again to get her attention with as little success. Leaning back in his Adirondack rocker, he followed the nun's view.

The Retirement Home for the Sisters of the Sacred Heart perched atop a wooded hill, its front porch an observation platform for the forest and gift shops lining the country road half a mile below. The wilderness of the past shoulder to shoulder with the tourist-friendly present.

The young nun who had guided Moser to Sister Dolorine made a kind of clicking with her mouth to signal sympathy. "I'm so sorry. It's like I told you, Detective. Sister has her good days and her bad days. We're having lunch inside if you'd like to join us?"

Moser paused. Was it his imagination or did he see the Sister's eyes flicker?

"No thanks. I'll just sit here a minute if that's all right."

"Of course it is. We love our Sisters to have as many visitors as possible. You know, even plants enjoy company. Call for me if you need anything," she told him as she retreated. "I'm Sister Jean."

"I might be a plant, but she's a pain in the ass," Sister Dolorine said quietly when the door closed. "If you want to talk, fine, but I'm not moving my head. If she sees me gabbing, she'll roll me in for leftovers, which is bad enough, but watching her trip to the Vatican slide show for the twentieth time is worse."

"I'd play dead too."

"Don't jump the gun. I'm not playing dead, just addled. Now, you want to know about Justin Ash. Let me think."

"It was a long time ago."

"Twenty years? That's a hiccup. He was four, maybe five when he came to us. He was one of the lucky ones."

"Lucky?" Moser repeated. "His parents were killed by his brother."

"That I don't remember. Their past we couldn't change, only their future. So, I'll stick to lucky. Maybe the couple who adopted him heard about his troubles and that's what decided them. Though I doubt that."

"How much can you remember about them?"

"You're trying to find him, then?"

The door to the porch swung open. Moser turned to see Sister Jean appear.

"Can I bring you coffee or tea, Detective?"

"No, thank you."

"Anything at all?"

"Scotch, if you've got it. Neat."

She laughed before returning to the house.

"His foster parents were horse people," Sister Dolorine told him.

"Horse people?"

"They owned a horse farm. It was something we talked about with the boy, so he'd get excited, you know, to go with them."

"Do you remember their names?"

Sister thought. "No. They might come back to me."

That I would get down on my knees and pray for, Moser thought.

"You said that *maybe* the couple knew about Justin's family history. Wouldn't they have had to?"

"Not necessarily," Sister said slowly. For the first time, Moser felt her pulling back. "Today, people want to know it all. Every detail about everything and everybody. It wasn't always that way. We had a policy of revealing a child's medical history, of course. But so far as the rest of their background, we were more, I'd say, general. Not inaccurate, but general."

"But you said that learning about Justin's troubled background might have influenced the couple to adopt him."

"I did. But that's how we referred to it. Both parents dead, but not—"

"Murdered," Moser completed. "If you revealed medical background, then you told them about Justin's brother, Michael? His mental problems? His commitment?"

"Mental illness wasn't looked on as part of a 'medical

history' then, Detective," Sister Dolorine admitted. "And it wasn't Justin's. I know what you're thinking, and you're right, of course. The Church has always had a large closet to lock away what they don't like to look at."

"And that wasn't the only reason Justin's brother wouldn't be brought up," she continued. "Sometimes, we found a couple wouldn't adopt a child if they knew the boy or girl had a sibling. They wouldn't want to separate them. So, no, we never spoke of brothers or sisters."

Moser thought about that. "Justin was five. Wouldn't he remember he had a brother?"

"He might. But at that age, after what he'd been through, Justin might have wanted to forget everything he could."

"Then it's possible that, even now, Justin has no idea his brother exists."

"Not unless his adoptive parents, or Justin himself, requested the information. That's state law, now. If his records haven't been computerized, he could wait till he's old as I am."

So Justin could be as clueless about Michael as I am, Moser thought.

"Justin's brother," Sister asked. "What's become of him?"

Moser recounted Michael's vanishing and the murder of Dr. Larkin that had brought him here to this porch.

Sister was silent afterward, thinking before she spoke. "You think Justin is in danger."

"I don't know. I don't know for certain if Michael's even trying to find him."

"But you think he is?"

Without a doubt, Moser thought. He remembered his last meeting with Michael. The talk, the tears, the shame.

His own.

He pushed the past away. "You said his foster parents were horse people. Do you remember where they lived?"

"I'm afraid not."

"Colorado? Texas? California?"

"I don't think so," Sister answered, tentative now.

That's all right, Moser thought. We've got forty-seven more states to go.

The porch door opened again. Moser was astonished to see Sister Jean emerge with a tray carrying a bottle of Coors Lite and a mug glistening with ice.

"Father Brennan likes his beer at lunch when he comes to say Sunday Mass," she confided.

Moser thanked her profusely as she put the tray down and then returned to the house. "Now I believe in miracles," Moser said as he poured.

"They do happen," Sister Dolorine assured them. "Recognizing them is the rarer thing. You're not going to drink that yourself."

"Are you asking me?"

"No, I'm not. You may have the mug, I'll take the bottle."

Moser put the Coors Light back down, half full.

"First things first, Sister. The state they lived in. The state that wasn't Colorado, Texas, or California."

Sister Dolorine was silent. Moser could hear the whoosh of cars from the road below.

"New York," she announced, pleased with herself.

"New York City?"

"No. No. But it was close to New York City. I remember the woman talking about it. She was lovely. They both were. She said New York City was 'close enough yet far enough' away."

"If I got you a list of towns, could you remember then?"

"I don't know, but I'll try. My beer?"

Moser handed her the cold bottle, raised his mug. "Cheers."

"Cheers." Mug and bottle clinked.

"Are you a Catholic, Detective?" Sister asked after drinking deeply.

"I was."

"What hurt you?" she asked.

Surprised by her choice of words, Moser hesitated before he answered. "Sister, I don't like to talk about it."

"I see. I should shut my mouth?"

"I'd appreciate that."

"After I say one more thing. A great benefit of being a Catholic is confession. It's not only a holy sacrament, it's cheaper than therapy. No matter what you've done or haven't done, God forgives. Of anything you might remember about your faith, I hope you will remember His love. He can forgive you."

Moser sat quietly, staring out over the trees. No, Moser thought. He couldn't.

And if He could, it would be the first time He was wrong.

CHAPTER 10

The Bedford, New York, farm he stared at from Blind Tom Road looked even more idyllic than the one Michael allowed himself to imagine.

Like people, places spoke to him without words.

A sense of peace—no, better—a sense of order came over him. A wash of gentleness, his mind rinsed of all uncleanliness.

There. Look down the dirt road leading to the large white farmhouse, the barns, the stables. Not even the loveliest lies he saw on television were as welcoming as this.

This is the world Justin, his brother, grew up in. This is the world Michael gave him.

He stopped and looked over the wooden fence to the gently sloping field of grass where a half dozen horses grazed. Michael loved horses. For a time, Bunyon Psychiatric took their teenage residents to a nearby farm for Equine Therapy. Residents would learn how to care for the horse they were assigned, and then, after four weeks of bonding, would be taught how to ride them.

Their counselors said the four-week delay was so that the horses would lose their fear of them. In truth, it was the opposite. Residents would feel a kinship by then, losing all fears about the riding lessons to come.

From watching countless old westerns on television, Michael already considered himself a good horseman who needed only a horse. He had studied the ones he saw on screen: Roy Rogers' palomino Trigger was even-tempered, while Dale's buckskin quarter horse, Buttermilk, was impatient standing still. The Lone Ranger's stallion, Silver, lived for adventure, and the temperaments of the horses of Bonanza's Cartwright men reflected their riders. Steady Buck, the Cartwright father's horse; Little Joe's spirited Cochise; Hoss's patient Chub. Their joyful *yee-haw* they called out with joy as they rode, fast as a bullet, toward their next adventure.

Michael's white draft horse, Gauntlet, was the largest and oldest in the stable.

It was Gauntlet's steady gaze that impressed him—the horse was sizing him up as carefully as Michael was him. Michael was impressed, too, by the horse's age. Gauntlet was 31. He had been subjected to the behavior of human beings, from indifference to cruelty, for what would amount to 93 years of a person's lifetime.

Michael couldn't wait for his weekly time with Gauntlet. He ran from the bus to the horse's stall. He fed him apples he collected all week from the dining room's fruit basket and watched Gauntlet loudly enjoy them, crunch after crunch.

Michael talked to Gauntlet. Quietly at first, but by week three he had told him about his brother, Justin, and the abuses of their father. As he brushed him, Michael made certain that his strokes were gentle and not affected by the rage that lived still within him.

He dreamed every night of riding Gauntlet. He was certain Gauntlet was just as eager, that he would welcome him in the saddle and break into a full gallop before the other residents had even one foot in their stirrups. In his mind, they sprinted faster and faster, outrunning their past, safe, the old world a blur, safe in their future where only they existed.

The week they would ride, Michael was told he had an "Assistant." Salvatore Ferretti was older than Michael and four times his weight. He was known to everyone as a thief of all that was edible, candy in particular. Residents receiving treats from the outside, or buying them in the institution's small store selling a selection of snacks, took care to eat them before Sal had a chance to search their room and eat them himself.

Sal's immense size should have made him feared, but although his nature was cruel enough, he was also a coward. Filled with anger, Sal was allergic to confrontation. He couldn't bring himself to face an enemy. A knife in the back was just as effective as one to the breast. Still, he knew it was a weakness, so his every act of aggression made up in malice what it lacked in face-to-face hostility.

Michael said nothing to Sal when the ranch head divided their duties. Later, he would learn that this was Sal's third relocation. Boys older than Sal refused to work with him. Those younger were found crying when they reached the bus to go back to the hospital. Since Michael spoke rarely and was not emotionally demonstrative, it was decided he and Sal might readily partner for the program's last weeks.

Michael disliked Sal instantly. He had seen him casually stretch out his leg to trip a resident carrying a loaded meal tray, and once observed him after lights-out standing over his sleeping roommate, pricking his arm, neck, and head with a needle. He speared his roommate's flesh carefully, gently, because he wanted to invade his dreams with pain, rather than startle him awake. He could stab longer that way.

Michael didn't want to put a comb or pick into Sal's hands. Instead, he added some hay to the bag of oats in Gauntlet's feed bag and handed it to Sal to put on. Neither boy spoke through the remaining hour they gentled Gauntlet and cleaned his stall, and went back to the bus to ride home without a word.

The next day, Michael was called to the office of the hospital administrator, Dr. Henry Granville. With him was Michael's current counselor, Dr. Ronald Larkin. To Michael, Dr. Larkin's dislike of him couldn't be more obvious if he wore a notice of it on a sandwich board.

"Michael, please sit." Dr. Granville waited until Michael did what he was told.

"Yesterday at the farm, how was your horse's behavior?"

Michael sensed Dr. Granville's question was direct and not accusatory, so he answered.

"He was good," Michael replied. "He's always good."

Michael saw Dr. Larkin look at Dr. Granville with a frown of disbelief.

"I'm asking, Michael, because Gauntlet was very sick last night," Dr. Granville continued. "He was having continual seizures. Fortunately, the vet pumped out his stomach before the chocolate in his system caused internal bleeding."

Dr. Larkin couldn't stop himself from attacking Michael. "Don't you know chocolate is toxic to horses?"

"Yes," Michael answered just as brusquely. "So is caffeine, tomatoes, and many houseplants."

"Did you feed any of those things to your horse?"

"No. That would be wrong. Gauntlet is a good horse," Michael answered simply.

"Salvatore Ferretti was helping you, wasn't he? Did you see Salvatore feed anything to Gauntlet?"

"I didn't," Michael told him truthfully. But even as he said it, Michael knew the boy was responsible. He had seen his bond with Gauntlet. Seeing any display of affection between them would be anathema to Sal since he had never felt it himself.

Michael spoke with no one for the rest of the day, ignoring anyone who addressed him. That night, he rose from his bed at 11:45. The staff was nearly finished their 8-hour shifts and were concerned mostly that their replacements would arrive on time or, even better, a few minutes early.

Michael reached Sal's bedside without being seen. He stood over him, made certain Sal was asleep, lifted the rock he had collected on the grounds, swung it over his head, and brought it down with all his strength on the boy's skull. Michael inspected the wound and was satisfied. He had aimed successfully at Sal's pterion, the "H" shaped meeting point of the temporal, parietal, frontal, and sphenoid bones. It was the thinnest point of the skull, according to his *My Body* textbook. At the least, Sal was unconscious. Michael now took from a paper bag the chocolate he had earlier found by scouring Sal's room. Once partially melted, he molded the six bars—two with peanuts—into a sticky brown ball. With his left hand, Michael pinched Sal's nose closed. When Sal opened his mouth to breathe, he shoved the chocolate glob into it, pushing it as far down his throat as possible.

Instinctively, Sal struggled, which Michael had both anticipated and relied on. Michael pulled Sal's flailing body to the edge of his bed, where he toppled over, landing heavily on the floor, face down.

Gripping Sal's hair, Michael pulled his head up as high as he could, then slammed his head into the floor again.

Done.

Someone on the new shift would discover Sal's body within the hour. Alarms would sound and an ambulance would be called. The subsequent investigation would later determine that the weighty Sal, probably nervous after being interrogated for poisoning a horse, would have calmed himself by massive overeating. He choked on the mass of chocolate in his throat and, finding himself unable to breathe, panicked and fell to the floor, causing head trauma.

Though Sal had no roommate to corroborate their theory—Sal's infrequent roommates stayed only briefly—the Administration would also assume that Sal was guilty of feeding Gauntlet the same, nearly fatal, chocolate. Sal's subsequent gorging would speak for itself.

———

"Hello!" Michael heard, and he left the past for the present.

A smiling woman on a horse rode across the pasture toward him. Fifty, maybe fifty-five years old, tall and lean, she wore jeans and a red flannel shirt. Her long hair was bunched at the back of her head but still hung halfway down her back, bouncing with the horse's movement.

Grey and white, her hair. Honest colors for a woman of her age. Michael approved.

When she spotted him, she smiled, and what a beautiful smile. Her teeth gleamed, her eyes welcomed. For a moment, a rush of feeling new to him took Michael aback. Is this anything like happiness?

"Hello," Michael returned. "I'm looking for the Trainor family."

"I'm Kate Trainor." She dismounted smoothly and closed the pasture gate behind her. "Can I help you?"

You have, Michael thought, her smile now on his face. You were my brother's second mother. My brother, who might now be inside your farmhouse, not two hundred feet away.

Michael couldn't stop sharing her smile, even when she stopped. All he wanted was to see Justin, to see him safe and happy. To see him once. Just once, and he would go away. And so, Michael lied.

"Have you ever ridden before?" Kate asked as they climbed the front steps.

"No," Michael answered, "But if I decide to relocate with my company, it would be something I'd like to learn."

"So, you'd be living—"

"Here. This is close to New York City."

"Amtrak runs trains through Bedford Hills and Mt. Kisco. They're close enough. But the commute's an hour plus each way."

"It would be worth it to live in an area as beautiful as this."

"I agree," she told him. "So did Paul, my husband. That's what got us here in the first place. This house, the acres we wanted, and the fact we're surrounded by a nature preserve, so nothing will change. I'm making coffee if you'd like a cup. We can sit here on the porch or talk inside."

"I'll come inside," Michael said.

Through the foyer, into the living room. Michael stopped at the fireplace, where Kate displayed her family with a series of framed photographs on the mantle. The largest, placed center was a family holiday pose. Kate Trainor, years younger, a man her age, husband Paul, and a six-year-old boy, all happy for the camera.

"This is Justin," she said proudly.

Michael stared at his brother. He was only a few months older than when he had last seen him, but he looked so different. Why? A moment later, he answered his own question.

He had never seen Justin so happy.

The phone rang in another room. Kate apologized and excused herself, leaving Michael to inspect the rest of the pictures.

This one, a big leap forward. Justin on horseback, now too

grown up to smile for the camera, a serious seventeen. Next to Justin the Horseman, Justin the Baseball Player. Nine? Ten?

Michael blinked, suddenly dizzy, so much rushing past him, the past as present.

Kate returned with Michael not even noticing.

"Are you all right?" she asked, touching Michael's shoulder.

She jumped back, automatic response, as Michael dropped to the wood-planked floor, felled by the weight of memories he never had.

Kate knelt beside Michael, calling his name, taking his hand and pulse. He was breathing easily, but still she rushed back into the kitchen for her phone.

A doorbell ring, then an immediate banging on the front door followed by a shouted "Hello!"

Holding the ringing phone to her ear, Kate hurried past the unconscious Michael toward the door.

Anton Mitzach had already let himself in, aggravated and impatient. Kate had never seen him otherwise.

"Mr. Mitzach, there's an emergency."

"Oh, yes!" he agreed, his Eastern European enunciation growing sharper as his volume rose. "Your barn is filth."

"We'll talk later," Kate snapped. The 911 operator picked up. "This is Kate Trainor at Bedford Hill Farm, 31 Blind Tom Road. A man here has collapsed—"

"I'm fine now."

Kate looked behind her, surprised to see Michael. "Are you sure?"

"I am." Michael stared past her at the still seething Mitzach. "It's nothing. I haven't eaten."

Kate thanked the emergency operator, punched off, and told Michael to sit and rest. She would feed him in a minute, despite his protests.

She turned her attention to business. "Now. Mr. Mitzach," she began, only to be interrupted.

"I wouldn't put pigs in that barn!" Mitzach announced. "Every time the same!"

"We muck out the stalls once a day and pick them out twice after that. I explained that to you last week."

"I know what you said," Mitzach countered. "I also know what I pay to board my horse in this shithole."

"I can give you a list of other stables," Kate suggested, but he had already gone, the screen door slamming closed behind him.

Michael hadn't moved.

"That's Anton Mitzach. He directs movies," Kate told him while staring through the screen door at her retreating client. "Thinks everyone is his extra. I've asked him to board somewhere else three times now, but he hears what he wants to. In the words of my sainted grandmother, the man's a 'Life Shortening Experience.'"

Something about Michael seemed different from before. His even temperament now seemed agitated, even angry.

"Come into the kitchen," Kate said. "You have to eat. After that, I can drive you to the hospital so a doctor can check you. It's only ten minutes away."

"I feel good," Michael assured her, his eyes still gazing outside at Mitzach. "I'm sorry I frightened you."

"It takes more than that," Kate laughed. "How about a sandwich? I have roast beef."

Michael thanked her. A sandwich would be a wonderful thing.

She stopped before reaching the kitchen. "In all this fuss I don't think I caught your name."

"Michael," he told her. "Michael Bailey."

———

THEY TALKED about everything in the world *but* riding lessons, Kate later realized. She took him through the history of Bedford Hill Farm from 1825, when her great grandfather had bought the two hundred fifty acres, to today, when the acreage had shrunk to fifteen, and she, his last direct descendant, ran it unassisted.

He shared her pride, and he shared her sorrow recounting her husband's death from a heart attack here, on the property, only two years ago. He understood, as she did, why their only son hadn't returned to run the farm with her. He was happy at his work. He had already left home to pursue it.

"And who can argue with happiness?" Kate said wistfully.

Kate left the room to get her son's most recent picture, taken two years ago at his graduation. Michael was excited again. College? Justin graduated from college? He was already proud of him.

"Here," she told him, returning with the framed picture. "This is Justin, last June."

Michael stared and said nothing.

"This was the day he graduated from the Academy."

The young policeman, smart in his new uniform, grinned at the camera.

A policeman. A policeman like the one who found them in the woods on the last day they were together. The same policeman he saw again, only a year ago.

"I want to hear about you," Kate was saying.

Michael was hesitant, but she was insistent.

Then it came to him. The sooner I tell her something she'd like to hear, the sooner all this will be over. The sooner he could find Justin.

With his hands curled around his coffee cup and his gaze

on the kitchen table, he thought back to his sessions with Dr. Cherry. The challenges she said he had, her analysis of emotions he didn't understand, but admitted to, without hesitation.

Dispassionately, he spoke of feelings of abandonment, waves of insecure causing his interpersonal challenges, ineptness, and finally, almost inaudibly, the fact that he had spent ten years in an orphanage where so many others had been chosen before they reached his age.

"But when you were adopted, were you happy with your new parents?" Kate asked.

Oh, yes. His life changed. They were perfect. Like Andy and Aunt Bee in Mayberry. Because they were, in fact, as real as Andy and Aunt Bee in Mayberry.

Kate laughed at the comparison but turned sincere. "When a child knows he's loved, it makes all the difference in his life."

Michael nodded, unsure of how to respond to such emotion. Only recently, he quickly continued, did he decide to find out who his birth parents were. He never would have done so when his adoptive parents were alive. Not after they had given him so much. He would never have taken the chance of hurting them.

"They would have understood," Kate assured him. "Believe me. Justin was adopted."

A thrill ran through Michael as Kate rose to refill their coffees. When she sat back down, she could feel vibrations from the floor. Michael Bailey's right leg bounced up and down like a piston.

"You told Justin he was adopted," Michael repeated.

"We never hid it from him," Kate explained. "Ever. We told him as soon as he got old enough to understand."

"When was that?" he pressed.

"Seven years, seven and a half. We were told he was from a very troubled family. He had lost both his parents."

"Did he remember them? Remember his family?" Michael held his breath.

"He said he didn't. The social worker we saw regularly said it wasn't uncommon. Especially after experiencing trauma."

"Trauma?"

"We asked for specifics, but the nun we met with said they didn't know more than that. Paul never believed her. I didn't either. Justin was withdrawn at first, but less so every week. It's true what they say about children. They're resilient. By the time he started pre-school, he was pretty much the person he is today. Outgoing. Optimistic. A good kid and a wonderful son."

"He was very lucky," Michael said.

"We all were," Kate insisted.

"Was he like me?" Michael asked. Kate looked confused. He hurriedly went on.

"Did he ever want to know more about his birth parents? His family?"

"No, not really," Kate answered. "He never seemed to care."

She saw on Michael's face a flash of emotion so brief to be unidentifiable.

"Justin's attitude is unusual," she quickly added. "Most adopted children are like you. They want to know. Some *need* to know. Paul and spoke to a psychiatrist about it. We were concerned Justin might be, well, suppressing things he didn't want to remember. But the doctor felt we were so open with him he felt less of a pressure to find his roots. That he would when he was ready. The 'don't fix what's not broken' philosophy."

She smiled, but Michael's smile seemed a second late.

"I hope you find what you're looking for," Kate said. "I'll pray you will."

Prayer was something Michael had no interest in. Michael's worldview was a simple one. Some people are well behaved, who live their lives without harming anyone else's. Good People, who deserved to live. The Bad People who hurt them deserve to die. It was that simple. He couldn't understand why anyone could complicate or confuse this. Michael needed no one to pray to, intercede, or pass judgment. Judgment was his own.

There had been enough talking. It was time to go.

"Thank you, Kate," he said as he rose from the kitchen chair. "You are a *very* good person."

CHAPTER 11

"What did you do to him?"

Anton Mitzach shouted at the stable hand, whose fingers were smeared with blood. In the stall, Mitzach's mare, Starlet, kicked again at her stall's wooden slats, the horse's eyes alive with anger.

This was one of those times Santiago chose to forget he knew English. He pointed to the deep scrape running from the horse's ribs to flank, glistening with a stream of blood.

"Arbol, nombre," Santiago insisted, gesturing back to the wound.

"Talk English, for Christ's sake!"

"What happened to her?"

"How would I know! She was fine when I rode her! She got hurt here! Cut herself on a nail or some goddamn thing. Don't think I won't sue."

Santiago gestured for Mitzach to stay calm. "Un momento." He left the barn to get antibiotics and Kate. Never had he seen a bigger horse's ass—and it wasn't Starlet's.

The director checked his watch, which was ninety seconds later than when he checked it before. Anxious to get back to the city for his latest casting session without a movie to cast, he had used his crop more heavily than usual. Ever since this MeToo nonsense had started up, finding actresses desperate enough to have a late-night dinner with him had become harder. But not impossible.

"Fuck!" he shouted with frustration at Starlet. Unlike people, these stupid horses didn't give a damn who you are. "I'm going! They're paid to take care of you! I don't have time for this!"

"No," someone agreed. "Life is short."

Mitzach turned. At the barn door was the man he had seen earlier in the farmhouse. The man slid the door closed behind him. The solid sound of wood slamming against wood reverberated.

"What did you say?" Mitzach demanded.

"You're a director. You make movies," Michael replied. "Which movies?"

Is he mocking me, Mitzach wondered? He was torn. Should he tell him to go to hell or tell him some titles?

Pride won out.

"*Slasher Beach*," Mitzach announced. "All three."

"I saw a slasher movie once," Michael said. "It was very bloody. But everyone around me was clapping and laughing. They fired the guard who brought it in for us to watch."

"The guard?" Mitzach stopped himself from asking. Jailbird or not, this man's a lunatic. A lunatic whose accent sounded very much like his own. Where is he from? Mitzach had changed his nationality three times since he had entered the United States.

"What was *Slasher Beach* about?" Michael asked.

"A slasher and the beach! What the fuck else? You got summer, lots of skin, and a nymphomaniac slasher. Made a fortune."

Michael said nothing.

"The higher the body count, the higher the fucking gross."
He turned from Michael and walked toward Starlet, but the
horse kicked out at his approach.

"Did you slash her?"

"What?" Mitzach faced Michael again.

"Your horse. Did you hurt your horse?"

"Fuck you!"

"You say that a lot. Fuck, fuck, fuck." Michael repeated the
word and every time the sound of it varied. He stood now by
the grooming tools hung on a barn post, brushes, and curry
combs. He reached for a hoof pick, its sharp end used to dig out
manure and stones caught in the horse's hooves.

Mitzach caught himself before instinctually responding.

"You make bad movies," Michael said. "And you hurt horses." He took a step toward him, hoof pick in hand.

"Who are you?"

Michael said nothing but now looked as discomfited as
Mitzach was.

Enough, this was more than Mitzach could stand. He was
boxed in between an angry horse and a Sunday School teacher.

"Fuck off," Mitzach concluded as he walked past him.

An arm grabbed his. The grip was so powerful it took a
moment to feel the sharp pain running down his arm where
Michael sliced through his shirt with the hoof pick, dragging it
across his skin.

"That's how your horse feels," Michael calmly told him.
"You treat it badly. Like you treated Mrs. Trainor, who is a very
good person."

"You're crazy!" Mitzach screamed.

Michael hesitated. "So?"

The blood was now seeping through Mitzach's shirt. But
not enough. Michael looked at the hoof pick, considering its

limitations. To Mitzach's surprise, he let go of his arm and handed him a nearby metal bucket.

"Clean her stall," Michael instructed him.

"*What the fuck?*" Incredulous, Mitzach looked from him to Starlet. The horse stared back, teeth showing. Starlet shifted to her right and left.

Michael pointed toward the horse with the hoof pick. "Clean it. Fucking *now*."

———

AT THE HOUSE, Kate opened her door to see Santiago holding his toolbox filled with veterinary first-aid supplies.

"His horse?" she asked, not needing his name.

"Si."

"Esta aldea es malisima con celebridades," Kate grumbled, reaching for her coat.

Santiago laughed. What she said was true. "This town is lousy with celebrities."

They set off for the barn, Santiago working to keep up with her. Halfway there, they heard screams and began to run. Yanking open the barn door, Kate and Santiago were stunned at the sight before them.

On his hands and knees, his left arm broken and his head bleeding heavily from a swipe of Starlet's hoof, Anton Mitzach scurried back and forth on the stall's floor, trying to escape her rage as he picked up clumps of her waste to throw in the metal bucket.

"Get out of there!" Kate screamed.

"Is he gone?" Mitzach shouted.

"Who?"

He rose, holding one side, but was immediately smashed

into the side of the stall by a brush with Starlet's haunches. As he dropped to the straw, Kate and Santiago rushed to stop the angry horse as she reared up over Mitzach, but not in time.

CHAPTER 12

MICHAEL SAT ON THE FALLEN TRUNK DEEP IN THE WOODS with his *My Body* textbook on his lap. Outside the barn, he had watched as Kate and Santiago dragged Mitzach from Starlet's stall. Satisfied, he began his walk to the road, spotting the sign for the adjoining trail and veering off through the trees.

Michael was sure the director had broken ribs with hematomas sure to follow but was curious about the damage to his left leg, abnormally angled. The horse's full weight must have come down to crush the femur, the strongest bone in the human body. Impressed at the horse's power, Michael wondered if it was Mitzach's tibia or fibula poking through his thigh.

Hearing an ambulance siren wailing in the distance, he looked up. They'd be looking for him by now on the roads and in the village. The solution was simple. Wait until night and it would be harder for them to see him.

About to return to his book, Michael saw a deer staring back at him from the edge of the clearing. Both stayed still. Michael sat for almost an hour until it came nearer, drawn by the smell of the orange peanut butter crackers he had bought earlier from a vending machine. In that hour, the deer and he watched a squirrel skitter across the fallen tree Michael was sitting on, grab one of the crackers laid out for the taking, then sprint back to its tree. A chipmunk skittered toward Michael, devouring cracker crumbs he had crumbled and tossed onto the dry leaves before him.

Sitting in the forest, Michael realized another reason Justin must have loved his new home so much. There were so many trees. Michael wondered if Justin remembered the Indiana trees behind their home. Trees were not only their playground but their refuge. For Michael, the trees had been a literal life-saver. Father and Mother always assumed when he ran out the back door that he sprinted deep into the forest for safety. Instead, sitting in his nearby treehouse with branches shielding him from view, Michael felt safe from any danger surrounding him. This self-protective instinct served him as well today as it did back then.

Michael noticed a rusty metal sign nailed onto a tree in the distance. "No hunting," Michael read. He looked back at the deer and nodded. He would be safe here. He liked animals. Very much. None had ever hurt him. More often, animals were victims of people. Like Starlet, the director's horse. Most couldn't protect themselves.

They were as helpless as young children.

CHAPTER 13

Harrisburg, Pennsylvania.

MOSER PULLED the Miata off the Interstate, stopping under the overhang of the hotel's front entrance.

He was grateful there was no valet in sight. After five straight hours stuffed into Peggy's tiny sports car, Moser would have to pry himself out. One overweight clown climbing out of the tiny circus car as the crowd smirked at his full body spasm.

Moser reached with his left hand to a lever near the car floor, pulling it up to allow the seat to recline a precious six inches. He rested, not wanting to move further, despite the banner hanging over the lounge entrance promising a happy hour that lasted one hundred and eighty minutes.

He had driven over three hundred miles since he last stopped for gas, leaving Flat Rock behind him today and Bunyon Psychiatric the day before.

Remembering his goodbye to Hayden, Moser knew his former partner felt he was running away. But there was a part of him that had never left Peggy's hospital or Michael Ash's institution.

The timer for the motel's billboard floodlights clicked on, illuminating their promises: *Free Continental Breakfast! Free Internet! Free Indoor Pool!*

Moser closed his eyes to rest them, and like a movie he could never turn off, the memory of his second meeting with Michael Ash at Bunyon Psychiatric continued playing.

In the hospital administrator's office, Moser and Hayden watched the previous night's iPhone footage with Dr. Granville. The boy and girl in the mini-movie were fifteen, sixteen at most. Naked, standing close, pale bodies still. In another time and place, both would be thought attractive. They stared at each other, eyes lifeless, unstirred by the sight of the other's body before them.

The camera shook slightly as its operator called out direction.

"Jason! Kiss her!"

Jason leaned over and pressed his lip to the girl's. Her eyes remained open.

"Tiffany, kiss back. Come on! Harder! Put your arms around him. Grab his ass."

Listlessly, Tiffany did what she was told.

"Okay. Jason? Hey! Listen to me! Reach out your hands... go on. Grab her. Grab one in each hand!"

Repulsed, Moser forced himself to keep watching. Command after command, the young people followed instructions. Step-by-step pornography with no pretense of passion.

The result was like that of a training film. "Lay down! Legs apart! Lick it! Suck it! In! Out!" Shaky close-ups of young, pale skin. Body parts moving sluggishly.

The coaching constant. The camera's eye closed in on Tiffany's face now filled with pain.

"Don't stop! Tiffany, scream!"

The scream was real. The picture went out of focus, the

sound of the camera hitting the ground, then darkness. When a picture returned moments later, it was a different one.

Now standing before the camera was Benny Weill, thirty-five years old and prematurely balding, filmmaker and Bunyon Hospital guard.

Distraught, standing on the red blanket, the light from the video camera now revealed their "set": the roof of the hospital.

"Hey, I'm sorry!" Benny apologized to the phone's camera. "Swear to God!"

The shot held steady now. Had the iPhone been placed on a flat surface, then turned on? But if that were so, how could Weill have instantly appeared a dozen feet from the lens rather than be seen walking from it? A timer? Or someone else was shooting. Tiffany? Jason?

"I'll erase it all, okay?" Benny promised. "Forget it happened, and I swear on my mother's grave I'll never do it again!"

Benny looked to his right. A glimpse of Tiffany, now with a shirt draped around her shoulders. Jason, then, must be the one filming.

Weill turned back to the camera now, his voice filled with more authentic emotion than anything previously seen on screen.

"We're okay, right?" Weill pleaded. "I'm sorry. It's all good."

Then the screen went dark.

Moser and Hayden turned to Dr. Granville. This was the second time they watched the iPhone film on the administrator's laptop, only hours after Benny Weill had been found dead in the hospital parking lot, four stories below the roof where he had been filming.

"You saw the blanket on the roof. We left it as is," Dr. Granville told them. "That's all we know." The good doctor hadn't pointed out that Benny Weill had landed in Granville's own parking spot, Moser noted. He wondered if there was anything else Granville was choosing not to mention.

"We know more than that, Doctor," Hayden corrected. "We know Weill was talking to someone, and we saw the girl at his side. So he was talking to the boy or someone else."

"How long has Weill worked here?" Moser asked.

"A year and a half. This kind of thing—" Granville pointed to his TV screen. "This has never happened before. Newton Brown, one of our guards, found the girl and boy on the roof after one of the patients heard the girl scream. Mr. Brown's outside waiting to talk with you."

"And the kids?" Hayden asked.

"Tiffany Baker and Jason Atkinson. You can meet them both, but you can see on the tape how heavily medicated they were. They're not much better now. I spoke to them before you got here and neither could hold a conversation."

"All Jason needed to do was hold was the camera and something to threaten Weill with."

"We found no weapons of any kind. On or off the roof. Maybe he had a good arm and threw it?"

"We're searching the area," Hayden said.

"What about the third patient?" Moser questioned.

"I'm sorry?"

"You said a patient heard Tiffany scream."

"Yes," Dr. Granville conceded. "I don't know if he'll speak with you at all. He's also on medication. A very disturbed young man."

"His name?" Hayden inquired.

"Michael Ash."

"Ash?" Moser repeated. He turned to Hayden. "I know him. Killed his parents and set their house on fire. Before your time." He remembered the boy sitting quietly in court at the defense table, never responding verbally or even physically to anything said from the stand.

"How old is Ash now?" Moser asked.

Granville read from the printout he held, gave a copy to each detective. As they scanned it, he carefully chose his words. "Detectives, as horrible as all of this is, we should keep in mind that Weill's fall was an accident. Weill and Jason might have scuffled, and Weill lost his footing. He could have even jumped himself, rather than face legal charges."

"When you decide what happened, let us know." Moser got up from his chair. "You can write the case up while we head out to lunch."

"I didn't mean to suggest—"

"That we don't have a homicide? That would make all of us happy, but for now? Why don't you concentrate on the lawsuits that will come from Tiffany and Jason's parents and leave the rest to us."

Hayden said nothing until he and Moser were alone in the corridor.

"You want to go back in and pistol whip him? Maybe it will put you into a better mood."

"All the guy cares about is PR."

"Really? A bureaucrat? Who'd've thunk it. What's wrong, Owen?"

Moser was dismissive. "I didn't get any sleep last night." That much was true. "How do you make this out?"

"It's all about who took the last footage. We know it wasn't the girl. She was standing behind Weill. It's possible somebody put the camera down and turned it on. The shots weren't jumpy. Maybe that kid you know has answers."

"Michael Ash. All Granville said was that he reported the scream. For all we know, he could have been Weill's film crew. The lab might tell us more than the kids can."

The detectives divided their work. Hayden would speak with Baker and Atkinson; Moser, the security guard and Ash.

Moser was glad to be busy. His lack of sleep and patience fueled him. It took less than ten minutes for the guard, Newton Brown, to admit Benny Weill had paid him to turn a blind eye on the filming and only seconds more to learn it was Weill's third session, the first two with the same girl but different partners, male and female. Brown had only sounded the alarm when Michael Ash reported someone screaming.

"Was Ash on the roof with them?" Moser asked.

"I don't know that," Brown answered, now bursting with cooperation. "He found me in the lounge. I was talking to another guard, Wayne Kerner."

And giving yourself an alibi, Moser thought.

"Hold on, you're thinking the Ash kid was part of this?" Brown asked. "No way."

"Why's that?" Moser asked, surprised at Brown's certainty.

Brown seemed surprised at the question. "Have you talked to Ash?" he asked Moser.

"Not yet."

"You'll see. Ash doesn't get involved with anything or anybody. He could be sitting in the cafeteria surrounded by a hundred other patients and he'd still be alone."

———

On his way to speak with Ash, Moser stopped in an empty lounge, pulled out his phone, and hit redial. "Peggy Moser, Room 210," he told the person answering. Another set of beeps, then a soft "Hello?"

He could barely hear her. "Hey, it's me. How are you feeling?"

"Just a little tired," she answered. "But at least I can nap. How are you?"

Only Peggy would ask that. He had spent his night in the chair by her bed, dozing when he could, while she spent her entire night in pain.

"Good. Hey, I'll be down there around six, six-thirty. How about I pick us up some real food?"

"Sounds good to me," Peggy replied. He could hear the smile in her voice. "We'll have a date. Bring candles and we'll light them in the bedpan. Give the room a nice, romantic glow."

They both laughed, wanting something to be funny.

"Any doctors come by?" Moser asked.

"Not a one. So that's good."

It wasn't. Both knew that. No doctors came by because there was nothing else to say.

"Owen? Did you think about what I asked you?"

"No time yet."

"That excuse is getting very old."

"So are we. Together. Okay," Moser said, "I'll see you soon. I love you."

"I love you, too."

Moser ended the call but looked at the phone, debating whether to call back. But then what? He'd only talk around the question that need answering.

———

BESIDES A FEW PENCIL SKETCHES, abstract or inept, taped to its cinderblock walls, Bunyon's arts & crafts room didn't have another art or craft in sight.

Moser stepped through the door, unlocked by an orderly. In the center of the room was a long table flanked by two dozen chairs, only two occupied. Michael Ash stared up at the ceiling while a nurse sat at the far end of the table, her arms crossed. Seeing Moser, she rose, eager to be relieved.

"Where's all the arts and crafts?" Moser asked.

"We keep them locked up," the nurse answered, walking past him.

Why should they get better treatment than anybody else, Moser thought?

He turned to Michael Ash, his back straight, hands folded together on the table before him. Moser glanced up to see what Michael might be staring at…

Nothing. A blank, white ceiling.

"Hello, Michael. I'm Detective Moser."

"I remember," Michael answered, his eyes still focused upward. "Owen Moser."

"You have a good memory. I'm glad to see that." Moser sat in the chair directly across the table from Michael. Black jeans, a white, button-down short-sleeve shirt. He was neatly dressed and groomed.

Normal.

"I'm hoping you remember what happened last night." Still no eye contact. "Can you tell me about it, Michael?"

"He took them to the roof."

"Benny Weill did?"

"Yes."

"Did he take you, too?"

"He made them take off their clothes and lay on the blanket," Michael went on, ignoring the question. "He told Jason to get on top of Tiffany. Touch her. Do things. He was filming them."

"Where were you during all this, Michael?"

"This wasn't the first time. He'd done this before."

"Did Benny Weill ever film you?"

"He knew what he was doing was wrong. He stopped his camera. He apologized."

"To who?"

Michael said nothing.

"And then what happened?"

"He died."

Michael lowered his gaze, looking for the first time directly at Moser. Only then did Moser remember the intensity of his eyes, locked onto his own as uninhibitedly as they did when he was eight years old.

"He died," Moser repeated. "How did he die? Did he jump? Did he fall?"

"He was not a good person."

"Does that mean he should have died? Good, bad. It's not that simple, Michael."

Michael stared back at him but said nothing.

"Most people don't see the world that way," Moser went on. "Things fall between good and bad. They're not black and white. They're gray."

"They're not," Michael replied.

"No?"

"What would happen if people couldn't tell black from white, or right from wrong? What kind of world would we live in? You're a policeman. You know."

Not long ago, he thought he did. Things were much clearer when he was certain what black and white looked like.

Michael stared at Moser, his expression changing as if he was filling with questions of his own.

"How is Mrs. Moser?"

Moser was surprised at first, not remembering that Peggy knew both Ash brothers from the school she taught at.

"She's good," Moser lied.

Michael's face now flushed. His eyes still focused on

Moser's. Michael's brows came together, then movement flickered across his lips.

Unsettled, Moser was about to speak but stopped himself. Michael's eyes began to fill. Was he about to confess to pushing Weill off the building? Was he breaking down?

"Detective Moser," Michael began. "Why are you so sad?"

Moser felt a chill. Staring at Michael, he was staring into himself and the desolation of loss Moser knew had already begun.

"My wife..." Moser's words were out before he could stop them.

Michael's hands unclasped now. He put them on the table and leaned in, focused on listening.

"She's sick. Very sick," Moser heard himself saying. "Lots of pain."

Michael nodded, "It hurts you when you can't help someone."

Moser remembered Michael's brother.

"Justin," Michael said at the same time. "Have you seen Justin?"

"No."

"Do you know where he is?"

"No idea."

"They won't tell me. That's wrong. He's my brother." Moser felt the power of Michael's frustration, as painful as his own.

"I'm sure he's fine," Moser offered, hearing its hollowness.

"No. You're not. He could need me. He could be in danger. I would do anything for Justin. Like you would do anything for Mrs. Moser."

For the first time since he had heard the word "cancer" spoken eighteen weeks ago, Moser felt tears come.

Michael Ash reached across the table and took both Moser's hands in his.

———

"Sɪʀ?"

Moser startled, his head hitting the convertible top.

"Can I help you?"

A valet leaned down, staring in the Miata's driver's window.

Moser ran his hand over his face, embarrassed.

"I'm good," Moser told him.

The valet was unconvinced.

"Are you checking in?"

Moser glanced at his gas gauge, then his watch. He could drive for at least two, maybe three more hours before pulling over. And the thought of being yanked out of his car by an 18-year-old kid decided him.

"I changed my mind. I've still got a while to go."

Moser put Peggy's Miata in gear and pulled out from the hotel canopy, not giving another glance at the banner promising the marathon happy hour.

Having six long months of happy hours behind him, Moser figured he could miss this one.

CHAPTER 14

"Close enough" to New York City but also "far enough away." That was as specific as Sister Dolorine could be about the horse farm of Justin Ash's adoptive parents. For some people, Moser thought, "close enough" would mean Antarctica.

Moser sat down on a chair he'd dragged to a small, lamp-lit desk in his relentlessly cheerful room at the Mount Kisco Holiday Inn. The bed was in sight, tempting him, but Moser pulled out the maps he had bought and the information he had gathered from the phone calls he had made in North Carolina, Virginia, New Jersey, and New York. One call for each gas stop.

He had gotten lucky on his second. Tom Cogger, of the New York Farm Bureau. Cogger told Moser that the three counties in the state that had the largest amount of horse operations were Duchess, Westchester, and Nassau.

"But that's now," Moser replied, looking for any way to narrow his search. "How many would have been operating twenty years ago?"

"I can tell you the count in Westchester, because that's where my farm is," Cogger offered. "Twenty years ago, there were nearly forty, I'm guessing fifty in Duchess and the same for Nassau."

Cogger volunteered to go back through the bureau's records, highlighting the older operations as well as their owners' names. The earliest he could do that? Next week.

"Mr. Cogger, I appreciate your help. But you know when you hear someone say, 'This is a matter of life and death?' This is one of those times." Moser stopped himself from adding, "no horseshit."

Cogger sighed before asking for Moser's number.

Moser thanked him and ended the call. He was still looking for a needle, but grateful for even a slightly smaller haystack. Then again, there was no guarantee that Ash's adoptive parents would have called him "Justin." He'd need to find every boy who was five at the time. And if Moser needed another thought to keep him up tonight, he realized Sister Dolorine's "close enough" expanse could easily include farms in New Jersey and Connecticut.

Spreading out a tri-state map, Moser swung a 60-mile radius from mid-town New York City with a pencil and thread from his most frayed shirt when his phone rang. Surprised, he picked it up.

"Hello?"

"News flash: you're not on the job anymore. You're an out-of-shape alcoholic. You better hope you don't find Ash."

"Steve. How's the family?"

"A kid outside D.C. picked Ash up hitchhiking. Said he robbed him. The kid's lucky Ash didn't do more than that."

"You're sure it was him?" Moser asked. Robbery? Something felt wrong.

"He identified himself as Michael, and his prints were all over the door handles. He's headed east. Get your ass out of New York and back home." Steve Hayden lowered his voice.

"Owen, listen to me. I know what's going on in your head. Not just Peggy, but how we handled Ash last year."

How "we" and not how "you." Moser was suddenly overwhelmed with gratitude for his partner.

"Still," he said, "I shouldn't have closed that case."

"I pushed you to. We both own this. What you're doing now, trying to find this guy on your own, it's stupid. And you're not stupid, Owen. That leaves only one reason I can see. Sacred Heart High School altar boy idea of penance."

"I'll come back, Steve."

Silence. "You mean that?"

"I do. And I appreciate you calling like this. Thanks."

Moser turned off his phone's ringer and packed what little he had removed from his suitcase. There was no time to waste.

If alerted, the Franklin PD could find him as easily as Hayden did tonight. Out of cash, Moser had only debit and credit cards that would leave a trail behind him.

He checked his map. The town Tom Cogger lived in was at most an hour away. He looked at the clock. It was nearly eleven p.m. Maybe Tom liked to stay up late.

Moser left his key on the bureau and took his bag.

He doubted his old partner believed he was coming back. They knew each other too well. At best, Steve Hayden would give him twelve hours before passing on his location to their Chief and the FBI.

———

A YEAR AGO, Moser had pulled free of Michael Ash's hands when he had reached across the table and taken his. Was that empathy? Or was Ash simply manipulating his emotions, diverting the reason Moser was interviewing him in the first place?

Moser had risen and walked across the room. He felt embarrassed for having broken in front of the younger man and more comfortable with a distance between them. He stared at the patient's drawings displayed on the wall, his back to Michael.

"How do you feel about what happened last night?" Moser began.

"How do I feel?" Michael repeated his words.

"About Benny Weill, Jason, Tiffany. Anything that happened, Michael. You don't seem to have any strong reactions."

"I'm not sure what I feel. Do you?"

Moser turned to him. "Are you glad Benny Weill is dead?"

Michael paused for a moment. "He was a very bad man. It's good he jumped. He can't hurt anyone else now."

"If Weill didn't want to jump, do you think it would have been a good thing for someone to push him?"

A pause before Michael answered. "It hurts to think. I asked them to switch my medications so I think better, but they haven't yet."

Moser returned to the table, sitting across from Michael. "Even on this medication, you still know who he was. Wouldn't you be a good man if you saved Tiffany and Jason from someone who wanted to hurt them?"

"I can't say," he finally answered, his face as unrevealing as Moser's. "There are bad people who deserve to die. And good people, like Mrs. Moser, who deserve to live. Isn't it the right thing to help them both?"

Moser called for an attendant to stay with Michael. He walked through the patient's ward. Through the window of the conference center, Moser saw Frank was still interviewing Tiffany Baker. She looked as wan and vacant as she did in the video.

Moser felt a desire to keep moving, as if activity could shake off the uncomfortable feelings that enveloped him as he talked with Michael Ash.

First stop, Ash's room. If Benny Weill was forced off the roof, it was because he was threatened with more than Ash's words. Assuming Jason Atkinson was as zombie-like as Tiffany Baker, then Weill faced some other threat strong enough to produce the panic Moser saw on the videotape.

Moser searched every piece of furniture in the room, every molding on the wall. He examined the mattress and the bed frame, noting it was sloppily put together. In one drawer, he found soap and deodorant. Ash was clean-shaven. Where was his razor?

Moser flagged down a nurse who told him patients used only electric razors that were given to them when asked for, then retrieved.

Moser climbed the stairs leading to the roof, pushing through the final fire door and stepping out into the sunlight. He tested the door to see if it would lock behind him. Finding it would, he took a pen from his pocket and put it between the door and the frame so it couldn't close.

He scanned the gravel-covered surface, walking toward the blanket he saw in the video, untouched afterward. Ten feet beyond it, Moser looked over the building's edge and found himself three floors above the parking lot Benny Weill had plunged to, now cordoned off with yellow tape. Moser turned back to the expanse of the roof.

So, then. Think.

Benny Weill is filming Tiffany Baker and Jason Atkinson. For some reason, he stops. Then what? Michael appears with a prophet's righteousness and convinces Weill to stop filming? Weill, shamed, makes an apology on camera, then dives off the building?

Back up, Moser told himself. Weill was a beefy man well over six feet tall. Tattoos on his neck, not a teddy bear. Twice Michael Ash's size and weight. Unless his assailant was even a bigger physical threat than Weill, why would he be afraid? Unless his attacker had a weapon.

But what? The medical examiner had found no wounds suggesting a gun or knife was used. If the staff here wouldn't fully trust patients with an electric razor, they weren't going to loan out hammers. And no one in their right mind would hand Michael Ash a baseball bat.

Go back to the filming.

Weill hears a sound behind him, any sound, the crunch of gravel, the roof's fire door opening or closing. He stops shooting, turns to face Michael, somehow armed. Did Michael attack or threaten him, coerce an apology and then throw him from the roof?

Moser didn't see any damage to Weill's face, no sign of struggle, even during his final close-up. Then again, maybe Weill wasn't hit on the face. At least until after his camera time.

He could already imagine his partner's first question: where's the weapon? What did Michael, or whoever attacked Weill, do with it? Throw it from the roof and take the chance of someone searching the grounds for it? Nothing had been found. Take the weapon with them, hide it somewhere in the hospital? The hospital could be searched and so could individual rooms.

Moser walked back to the roof's entrance, put his pen back in his pocket, and climbed down the stairs to wait for his partner in Michael Ash's room.

"Zip times two," Hayden reported minutes later. "Both those kids are floating in a universe many drugs away from our own. Tiffany doesn't remember being raped, let alone being on the roof. Jason remembers nothing but the Hershey bar Weill gave him. How 'bout you and Ash?"

"He's a smart kid, no matter what he's on. He could have threatened Weill," Moser said.

Moser saw Hayden frown and knew why.

"So Ash tells that tattooed mountain of fat to confess, then orders him to jump, and he does?" Hayden countered. He saw a nurse peer into the room as she walked down the hallway and closed the door before saying more.

"Tell you what. While you're looking for a grand jury to believe Ash killed that kiddie porn waste of skin Weill, I'll dig out one of my bowling trophies. Because even if Michael Ash is charged, the public will want to give him an award, not a trial."

"I hear what you're saying—"

"Do you? A psychopath throws a kiddy pornographer off the roof. Tell me who's going to get all worked up over that?"

The sarcasm in Hayden's voice was gone now, replaced by earnestness.

"What's the point, Owen? Even if we found a weapon, we'd end up throwing money at a trial that would do one thing: switch Ash's jail cell from here to County Correctional."

Moser looked at his partner. "Did you talk more with Dr. Granville?"

"No point. You heard him this morning. He's going to fight anything we call this but 'suicide.' He'll run to everybody, from the captain to the County Board. And I'll tell you now, they'll back him a hundred percent."

"So we let them make our calls for us?"

"Owen, we make calls every day. But you make calls as Detective Third Grade. I'm still at First. I'm not going any higher by pissing off the wrong people. And with this, some scumbag who *should* get thrown off a roof, I won't lose sleep. My call's made."

Moser's phone rang. He was momentarily grateful for the interruption until he saw who was calling. Moser answered, listened, and after a few words, tucked the phone into his back pocket. "That was the hospital. They want me down there."

"I'll drive," Hayden said, following Moser down the corridor.

"First time they called like this," Moser said as they reached their car. He didn't have to say more. They drove in silence to St. Mary's.

Too many decisions, Moser thought. Decisions about Peggy and cancer. Decisions about Michael Ash, a man with no self-doubt, no regrets, maybe not even a conscience.

"There are some people who deserve to die," Moser heard Ash's words again. "And other people, like your wife, who deserve to live."

He had made his call on the case even before Hayden had made his own. At no point did Moser feel compelled to tell him that earlier, looking under Michael's bed, he noticed one of its mattress' support slats was missing.

CHAPTER 15

MICHAEL HELD OUT HIS ARM, THUMB EXTENDED. AT FIVE a.m., there were few vehicles, but Michael didn't see the empty highway. In his head, he saw the photograph of his brother on the day of his graduation.

Michael felt it was more than a picture he'd been handed. It was a message from Justin. Justin, posing proudly in uniform, Kate and Paul beaming on either side of him.

Michael had stared at the picture, committing every detail to memory. It was practice for what he'd need to be doing soon when he'd set actual eyes upon his brother.

One look, Michael swore to himself for the countless time. One look that must last him for the rest of his life. He would see his brother, there, before him, working, happy with himself and his place in the world, and Michael would be happy too.

One look, but not a single word, and Michael would move on, never looking back. Highway 684, south to White Plains, then on to New York City.

Michael waited patiently, as proud of his brother as Kate and Paul Trainor had been. Justin Ash, a graduate of the New York City Police Academy.

Justin Ash in full uniform.

Justin wearing his policeman's badge, #72487. A badge as good as any map. Michael would find out what all its numbers meant, then find his brother.

He saw an SUV's brake lights go on. The driver slowed down, stopping to give him the ride he needed. New York City, and his brother, were only 57 miles away.

Michael climbed into the front passenger seat of the Chevy Tahoe as a voice on WQXR announced the overture for Mozart's *Impresario*.

Michael enjoyed Mozart. He enjoyed all music and the sensations that sank into him as he listened.

"Good morning," said the SUV driver with a smile.

"It is," Michael agreed, returning it. "It will be."

ACT TWO

"In uncomplicated cases of transference, neurosis, the ego, reacts to anxiety and the dangers to which it feels exposed... a threat of emotional or physical abandonment... fear of the loss of love..."

"Now he discovered that secret from which one never quite recovers, that even in the most perfect love one person loves more profoundly than the other. There may be two equally good, equally gifted, equally beautiful, but there may never be two that love one another equally well."

CHAPTER 16

THE CHILDREN'S PLAYGROUND OVERLOOKED NEW YORK City's FDR Drive, a constant rush of cars racing north and south along the eastern edge of Manhattan Island.

Edward Chen, a man in his late twenties, pushed a wheelchair occupied by an elderly man, to the center of the children's playground. Both men looked out of place, more likely to be seen on Wall Street than surrounded by slides and colorful polyurethane animals mounted on springs.

The elderly man in the wheelchair, a gray blanket covering his legs, squinted through thick spectacles and ran his hand over his thick white hair. Seated on a bench across the playground were two women caregivers gently pushing baby carriages back and forth.

Two more childless men approached the playground, both dressed casually. Chaz, the taller man, slowly scanned the area, then stood at the playground's gate. A muscular man in his twenties with a ponytail pinned up on top of his head, the two women stared at him openly, quietly sharing their assessments.

Finn, the shorter new arrival, continued toward the two men at the center of the park. His scalp was shaved, so the headset he wore to communicate was more visible than the one worn by his long-haired colleague. A Frankenstein-like bolt was tattooed on each side of his neck.

"You go now," he told Edward Chen.

"Mr. Kass needs me," Chen insisted.

Kass, in the wheelchair, looked from Finn to Chaz, then raised his hand.

"I'll be fine," Kass told him. "Wait in the car."

Reluctantly, Chen obeyed, making eye contact with the pony-tailed Chaz as he exited the playground and walked to the double-parked limousine a half-block away.

Finn, though shorter, still had to look down to address the seated Kass. "Phone. Don't move. I'll look."

Kass sat rigid as Finn quickly ran his hands over and under his coat and suit, retrieved a cell phone from his pocket, then continued down his legs to the shoes. Circling the wheelchair, Finn checked behind and under it for anything concealed.

"Heads up," Finn shouted to his companion. Chaz caught Kass's cell phone. Hands now free, Finn then put one hand around Kass's chest and under his arm, lifted, and skimmed his free hand across the wheelchair's seat. Across the playground the stroller women stared at them, all conversation stopped.

"People are watching," Kass protested.

"You want to sell tickets?" Finn asked. He stepped back, satisfied, adjusting the microphone curled around his ear. "All clear," he reported.

A half-mile away, a taxi headed south on the FDR changed lanes to take the exit within sight of the playground. The man in the back seat was dressed in all things Armani: suit, shirt, even gloves. He, too, wore a headset. "Three minutes," he answered.

With his aristocratic features and every hair in place, Vincent Krelik looked misplaced in the taxi's worn back seat. He leaned forward and spoke in Russian to Otts, the cab's driver. Otts nodded. Otts felt shamed behind the wheel of this rusted ruin on wheels instead of his pristine Mercedes. Checking access to his gun holster slightly lifted his mood.

Kass and Finn were no longer the center of the caregivers' attention. Once Chaz had smiled at them, they no longer cared why he was here. Whatever it was, they were on his side.

"A good place to meet," Kass observed. "Your boss is a clever man."

Finn couldn't stop himself. "My idea," he told Kass.

"Really."

"Nobody wants to see kids get hurt."

"Ah!" Kass observed. "A man of compassion."

The taxi signaled right, turning off the exit, driving slowly up the street toward the children's park. Kass watched it pull to a stop outside the playground gates. Chaz darted a look behind him as the back door to the cab swung open and Finn began to push his wheelchair across the blacktop.

Kass tried to see into the dark back seat: a well-dressed, strong-featured man whose gleaming hair caught what little light there was.

What happened then was simultaneous. A shout from the cab's driver and its door shut. Chaz reached for his gun as Finn stopped the wheelchair and went for his.

The cab spun a U-turn on the one-way street, on and off the sidewalk, then sped back the way it came, passing cars coming off the exit ramp as it accelerated back onto the FDR.

As Chaz swung his gun toward him, Kass jumped from the wheelchair, spun to grab Finn behind him by his windbreaker, then pulled him forward as a shield. Chaz's first shot killed Finn on impact.

The two women from the bench already had reached into their strollers and pulled out their weapons. They hit Chaz twice before he could fire his second shot.

Maria Rodriguez, one of the two "caregivers," ran to Kass. "You okay?"

Kass pulled off his mustache and wig of white hair, revealing Detective Justin Trainor. "Yeah, I'm fine," Justin assured her as he scanned the playground. His partner, Det. Edward Chen walked toward him while Dorothy Mead, the second undercover caregiver, called for an ambulance and support.

"What spooked them?" Chen asked Justin, scanning the apartment buildings surrounding the children's park. "Was somebody lookout?"

Justin picked up Chaz's headset, now a few feet from his body.

"There was nothing to see," Justin answered. "Whoever called knew what was going down and called them just in time."

"One of us?" Chen questioned. "Nobody knew."

"Somebody did," Justin replied. "Everything we can do is useless until we find out who."

CHAPTER 17

MICHAEL STOOD AGAINST THE WALL OF THE APARTMENT building, stiff with terror. Arms outstretched, eyes closed, his face and palms pressed to the brickwork. He tried to block out the stream of cars on his left and the crowd of people to his right swarming up the stairs rising from underground.

Ten minutes earlier, he had stepped from the car that dropped him at the corner of 81st Street and Central Park West. The elderly man with tufts of ear and nose hair who gave him this last ride hadn't stopped talking from the rest stop on the Hutchinson Parkway until now, when he pulled over and let him out.

Michael was grateful the driver only needed a body in the car for his audience. He spent the trip staring out the window, certain they were traveling faster and faster. He glanced at the speedometer. No, it wasn't the car. He turned back to the endless traffic shooting past them, at them, held back only by the highway divider.

The car passed the George Washington Bridge and Michael looked out onto the Hudson River on his right.

"Boats," Michael said out loud, surprised.

"Garbage scows," Nose Hair said. "You know how many tons of garbage they haul out every day?"

Michael half-heard, staring through the front window as they merged into the traffic of the Westside Highway. A huge hospital and apartments to his left, the river to his right, Michael found his heart racing.

Breathe slowly, he told himself. Do not let your body betray you.

Building after building, block after block, each block twice the size of Bunyon Hospital's entire grounds. It was as if all the world's cities had been compressed to fit into these 325 square miles of Manhattan.

Michael stared at billboards selling whiskey and extolling safe driving, but his mind had already left the car. He was outside, rushing through the streets, searching for Justin and finding him looking proud and happy in his uniform. Justin, standing tall, hands on his hips, sensing their connection the moment he and Michael saw each other, throwing his arms around him, a hug that would never let go. Justin, telling him over and over, "You found me, Michael. You found me."

No.

Michael stopped himself. That will not, cannot, happen. He cannot allow himself to get that close, to speak, to reveal himself. For his brother's sake. As long as he's happy.

Off the highway now and into the city itself. Michael felt he was speeding across the bottom of a canyon, overwhelmed by the immensity of the structures around him, over him, and the torrents of people engulfing its streets.

Michael didn't even realize when the car had stopped. Nose Hair stared at him, anxious now. How long had they been parked?

"You did say the West Side?" the man asked, dubious.

"Yes," Michael answered, having no recollection of speaking.

"This is it. I'm going through the park to the East Side now."

"I'll get out, then. Thank you for your ride."

"Good luck, son." The man sounded sincere, as if Michael would need it.

Michael stepped out of the car's cocoon and into the chaos, the blur of movement, people speeding past and around him, more faces and frustrations, more energy than Michael had ever felt before.

A traffic light on a pole and a subway stop, people walking up and down from stairs leading underground. A dozen feet away, the canopied entrance of the stately Beresford Building. He rushed to the building's wall, bumping through the stream of subway riders, and clutched onto the granite structure for support, to slow his head from spinning.

He had to move. He knew he was the only person in this city standing still. Slowly, he released his grip, turning to put the building at his back.

Across the street stood a gigantic structure with a glass wall and a slope of steps at its entrance. Flags flew, declaring it a museum. Museums were like libraries. Michael knew that from television. People sitting and staring quietly, silent and well behaved. A place he could catch his breath and let his thoughts slow down.

Stepping off the curb, he focused on crossing carefully between the painted lines on the street, ignoring the beeping cars braking around him.

On the sidewalk, Michael increased his pace, walking quickly past person after person, focused on the museum steps ahead. As he reached them and climbed, an army of children burst through the building's doors, shouting triumphantly as if having escaped... well, a hospital.

Michael stopped, letting them rush past, followed by a tour group, their leader shouting in Japanese. Michael turned, almost colliding with an Asian man followed by three women wearing silk robes, when across the street he spotted trees.

Woods.

Safety.

Michael waited impatiently for a break in the traffic before him, then ran for the shelter of a familiar green world.

It was Central Park, a sign told him. Men and women of all ages strolling, sitting on benches, some simply staring ahead as they did on the grounds of the hospital.

Youthful laughter. Michael looked and saw a fenced-in children's play area. A plaque proclaimed it the *Diana Ross Playground.*

Diana Ross. Michael tried to place her. Yes, another image from the TV screen. A singer, very beautiful, huge eyes, lush black hair, and gowns that sparkled. Had she pushed her children on these swings?

Ahead, a car on a service road. Park Police. Michael hailed them, running toward it as the car stopped.

"Help you?" asked the officer driving.

He could. Yes. There was a New York policeman he wanted to contact, a friend from the past. Michael gave his brother's name and badge numbers.

The policeman nodded. Two of the numbers designated precinct. The policeman gave him even more numbers, street and address, which Michael committed to memory even before the police drove on.

His brother was close to him, Michael felt that. Here, in the same city, possibly only minutes away.

Michael's head throbbed. His fault. He had left all his pills behind.

"Hey!" A shout from a helmeted man on a bicycle. Startled, Michael retreated from the path.

Even here in the park, amid trees and benches, people moved faster than videos on fast forward.

Seeing a sign that said *Swedish Cottage Marionette Theater*, Michael followed its arrow to the wooden building, then opened his arms, flattening himself against it, shutting his eyes to still his thoughts.

Marionettes. He had made one once, tying strings to the head and feet of Justin's one-eyed bear and attaching them to the short branch he used as a control stick. Justin laughed when he made the bear dance for him. Michael sang, bouncing the puppet back and forth across the wooden planks of their treehouse, their hiding place.

Michael had found the abandoned deer stand when he was seven and it was winter, trees bare, revealing slats nailed to a trunk leading to a platform thirty feet above.

To him it was a castle, though it had only three walls, its flimsy steps serving as a moat so no one bigger than he could hope to reach him. A sanctuary where he could sit, silent and invisible, watching the back door of his house when his father emerged, shouting for him, searching only the ground with his eyes. Not finding him, he would climb into the rusty Ford truck and drive away.

Later, sometimes hours, his mother would emerge, standing on their back step, her arms folded, hugging herself.

Michael knew then he could climb down from the castle.

Not once did she ask where he hid. Not once would she even look at him when he walked by her. He would return to his room, knowing days would go by before they would talk again.

He helped Justin climb to the castle when he was only three, despite the danger. There were worse dangers behind them in the house. Justin must learn where to be safe and how to be so still he became part of the tree.

Justin cried, afraid of the height, but Michael never stopped talking, reminding his brother of the peanut butter sandwiches they could soon eat in their secret hideaway.

Step-by-step Justin climbed, Michael behind to coax and catch him, until they reached the last step and stretched out on the wooden floor, feasting on peanut butter and watching the one-eyed bear dance with joy at the sight of them.

Later, unafraid, Justin would look down from the tree without covering his eyes, seeing their house, seeming small now from where they sat. And they were bigger, taller, so much more powerful. How could they have ever been afraid of anything, anyone, so tiny?

Justin came to the castle often, then.

He had come on their last night together when Michael ran out the back door, followed by his father's threats and curses. They were lucky that night, both he and Michael. Their father shouted into the forest, unwilling to follow his son from their yard into the darkness.

Halfway up his ladder, in the light spilling from the kitchen, Michael saw Justin push open the back door, unseen, unheard over their father's shouts.

Careful, Michael whispered, as he waited for his father to turn and spot his brother, waited for Justin to call out for him, unable to find him in the dark, a call that could cost them their safety and their secret. But Justin ran across the yard behind their father's back, vanishing into the woods.

Michael leaped to the ground, running toward where his brother vanished. Finding each other, they retreated to their haven, watching their father below, too small now to catch them.

Now, standing at Central Park's Marionette Theater, Michael realized he wasn't shaking anymore. Memories of Justin always calmed him more than any pills or needles could.

He lifted his hands from the wall of the Swedish Cottage and turned to face this world of a city, bracing himself.

The park seemed quieter now. Even better, not a single person paid him any attention. They walked or rode or ran on their way as if he wasn't there, as invisible as he once was as a child, concealed by leaves and branches.

CHAPTER 18

"So, we blew it big time. That's what you're telling me?" Chief William Bolger faced Justin Trainor, Detective First Class and head of his Undercover Squad.

Justin offered the only good news he had. "None of our guys got hurt. And we might learn something when we investigate his two shooters."

"If we can trace them," Bolger snorted. "And you couldn't make their boss."

"For a positive I.D.? I didn't get close enough."

"You sure as hell didn't." Chief Bolger stared down at his desk. It was a stare Justin knew. What he thought couldn't get any worse would.

"Look, Justin. I just spent two hours swinging dicks with the DEA. They've got a lot of questions."

"How about asking them some?" Justin countered. "Like why didn't they move fast enough to cut off his cab when they had four cars for back up. We rolled the minute Kass got the call for this meeting. We had our people suiting up before anybody knew what hit them. Nobody even got briefed till the ride over."

"Okay."

"So nobody knew how it was going down. Nobody had prior notice. Nobody but you, me, and the DEA. Who scared them off? Us or them?"

"Save the outrage, Detective, I'm not done yet." Chief Bolger took a breath. "Six months' work for one meeting and that went to shit. The Bureau's sending somebody from D.C. to 'supervise' the case. You've got to meet with him and hand over everything you got. If it means anything, you went by the book and that's how I'm writing it up. Meanwhile, have Pinkney sketch up whatever you remember from the guy."

"It will be useless."

"Then get a useless sketch. We're done here."

"This is all bullshit politics."

"Everything is. You don't know that by now?"

Rather than speak his mind and regret it, Justin walked to the door.

"Trainor!"

Justin turned back to the Chief.

"The beautiful thing about pessimism is that you can only get happily surprised."

Edward Chen barely waited for Justin to close the Lieutenant's door before descending. "Tell me."

"The DEA is taking over."

"Goddamn!" Chen's anger flipped to worry. "What did he say about me?"

"He thinks you're dreamy. Did Kass call?" They walked down the fire stairs rather than wait for the elevator.

"His wife did. The DEA briefed her and Kass, mentioned you got a look at the guy. Now they're both freaked. She wants round-the-clock police protection."

"They'll probably get it," Justin predicted. "Even though their penthouse has tighter security than Tiffany's." He pushed through the precinct's front doors onto the sidewalk. Reflexively, Chen pulled out his cigarettes and lit one.

"You've seen Mrs. Kass," Chen said. "The old man's protecting his assets. Me, I think the biggest threat to his health is watching her undress every night."

"What can I tell you, friend? Maybe we should have gone into big pharma."

"That's my parents' fault," Chen complained. "They always told me to keep away from drugs."

"Same here," Justin said. "Christ, mine would have killed me."

CHAPTER 19

The tall, well-dressed woman strode through the lobby of the St. Regis Hotel directly to the elevators, stepping into the first to arrive. Despite her briskness, she knew that every man and woman she passed stared or pretended not to.

Rebecca had always been attractive, but since her teen years, she examined her face and body in the same way a shrewd realtor sized up a piece of property. What existed was a solid foundation, but with a series of small, cosmetic improvements, she could more than double the sale price.

Suite 1015.

Getting off at the tenth floor, she stopped before a mirror in the foyer and toyed with her hair, waiting for the next elevator to arrive, then the one after that. A mother and her teenage daughter. A Japanese couple. No one else.

Comfortable now, Rebecca walked down the carpeted hallway to her suite of rooms, entering with a swipe of her key card. Overlooking Central Park, the windows of the parlor offered picture-perfect postcards of a New York autumn.

She wasn't here for the scenery. Tossing her coat on the nearest chair, Rebecca kicked off her heels and walked directly into the bedroom, unhooking her dress and letting it drop to the floor.

Reaching down to pick it up, Rebecca was off balance when he grabbed her, coming fast from behind the door. He pushed her forward onto the king-size bed, pinning her down with his weight as both gloved hands wrapped around her throat.

She tried to breathe but couldn't. Releasing one hand from her neck, the man ran it down her body, then between her legs, tearing off her flimsy black lace panties.

He flipped her over, one hand still clutching her throat, then abruptly released her.

Gasping for breath, she stared up at the man still kneeling over her. Her hands rubbed her throat as she tried to speak. "Why did you stop?"

"I'm taking my time. You've fucked me once today already."

Rebecca sat up in bed. "I had no idea Leon went to the police. They had his phones tapped."

"He tells you nothing?"

"He told me everything at first. You know that. I encouraged him. I said he should meet you."

"And now?"

"Now is today. I thought everything was on track until he walked in with the police. There was no way I could warn you. I asked why he didn't tell me. He said he didn't want me to worry."

Rebecca was standing now, the bed between them.

"Were you followed here?"

"No. I'm sure of that." She pushed her hair back. "He doesn't know about us."

Vincent Krelik studied her. "Doesn't it upset you that your husband won't discuss his work with you?"

Rebecca looked at him. "I don't think he married me for that." She waited for him to come to her. Sooner or later, she knew he would.

"One of the policemen saw my face," he said.

"Which? I met two," she said.

"Only one identified me." He took from his pocket a copy of the police sketch made of him and handed it to her.

"How did you get this?" she asked. Rebecca looked at the sketch and then smiled.

"They might as well have drawn a stick figure. Do you recognize this man?" she asked as she handed it back. "I don't. And I certainly wouldn't sleep with him."

She was right. The sketch could have been any white Caucasian male with two eyes, ears, a nose, and a well-cut head of hair.

Rebecca saw him relax now. Krelik was still fully dressed in his coat suit and gloves. She tucked the tips of her fingers over his belt between his pants and shirt.

"Do you know the fortune we might have made?" he asked.

"You have one already. So does Leon. So, will I, sooner or later." Rebecca unbuckled his belt. "And I'd say sooner."

"Still," he began but was stopped by her mouth and tongue.

"That's what I like about you," she said, releasing him. "Nothing's enough."

Back on the bed, clothes scattered, bodies moving, tight together. He reached for her neck again. One hand, then two. He felt her excitement, then her fear and thrashing fury as she realized he wasn't letting go.

Krelik waited, keeping his grip for minutes after Rebecca stopped struggling, and then searched for a pulse. Finding none, he removed her wedding ring.

He examined the room as he dressed, picking up the police sketch that had fallen to the floor. He was unconcerned about fingerprints, and any fiber samples would never be matched to the gloves he would destroy.

Krelik opened his small suitcase, putting in it all Rebecca Kass had brought to this room: her clothes, her coat, her handbag. Looking out the suite's peephole and seeing an empty hallway, Krelik exited, hanging a "Privacy" sign from the outer doorknob as he pulled it closed.

One less person who could link him to Leon or Rebecca Kass.

Walking to the elevator, he kept his head down, aware of hotel cameras positioned in the hallway and elevator. Riding down, only one thing disturbed him. Despite long odds, the disguised detective had glimpsed him.

He would protect himself by eliminating him, Krelik decided. He saw no other alternative.

There was not only beauty but safety in the details.

CHAPTER 20

Bridget Lee painted a thin brushstroke of vivid red across the portrait already on her canvas. Attractive and as vibrant as her work, Bridget stepped back to examine it.

"What do you think?" she asked.

"The red streak across his face makes the guy look like a cutter," Justin replied.

"A cutter?" She pointed her brush at him, advancing as Justin stepped back, raising his hands in surrender.

"I'm artistically disabled! You know that."

"At least you don't fake it, you get points for that. Now don't think, just tell me your first reaction."

Justin nodded toward the portrait. "I don't trust him."

"Him? He's you! What do you see?"

Beside the easel on the wall were taped a dozen photographs of Justin's face from all angles.

"A man bloodied, unbowed, and cut off crotch high."

"Go for the joke. Avoid your real feelings."

"To what? This guy who's who looks angry? Dangerous?"

"Not dangerous," Bridget insisted. "Enigmatic."

"Enigmatic?"

"Half here, half somewhere else you never talk about."

"Classic cop behavior. Hey, I gave you the Owner's Manual."

"Classic avoidance."

"I've got nothing to say! Bridge, how many times do I have to tell you that? I'm not a complicated guy! If that's what you want—"

"I want you. But *all* of you." She kissed him.

"You think so? You're painting *that* picture and dating the only guy in this city who's not on a psychiatrist's couch."

"It's never too late." Bridget kissed him again. "You want my appointment tomorrow?"

"I want you to take off your clothes."

Bridget stripped off her paint-covered jeans and t-shirt at record speed. "See that?" she said, as Justin hurried to catch up. "I'm very accommodating."

"What would I say to a shrink?" Justin asked, kicking his shoes off.

"You could complain about me, vent about work or, God forbid, find something out about yourself."

Justin tossed his shirt to the floor before the canvas. For a moment he was still, staring at it once again.

"What if I did go to a shrink?" he asked Bridget, "and I found out I don't like me?"

CHAPTER 21

MICHAEL FOCUSED ON THE SIDEWALK BEFORE HIM, navigating around the legs of anyone approaching. It was the only way he could lessen the assault in his head. Too many faces saying too much. Too many eyes and mouths, squints and slouches that spoke to him.

Darting a look at the street sign, then side glances to follow the numbers on the buildings, Michael finally stopped and raised his head to stare up at a sign over a doorway announcing itself as the 56th Precinct, his brother's workplace.

Michael's plan had changed again, the latest idea in the countless he had formed in over seven thousand days of confinement.

This plan was better. He made it on the outside.

Rehearse it again.

"Officer Justin Trainor, I'm Michael Bailey. I don't want to take much of your time," he'd begin.

Justin would be watchful, listening.

"I just met your mother up in Bedford. I don't think I've ever met a parent prouder of her child than she is of you. Proud of who you are and what you do. I just had to tell you that. And when I passed this building and saw the precinct number—"

Shake your head, acknowledge the coincidence, and continue. "I said to myself, that's a sign. I've got to go in and tell him. Meet him. I hope I'll be just as proud of my own son."

Justin would be smiling now, putting out his hand to shake his, thanking him.

Thanking him.

Then Michael would let go of his brother's hand, one he held so many years ago, and he would say goodbye for the last time.

Good, Michael thought. He took out his wallet and carefully removed the old picture on the newsprint he had encased in plastic. November 1, 1990. There had been a headline and a story about the fire, but he had long discarded the rest of the paper. It was a picture cropped from a class portrait. Staring at the camera were two smiling boys: "Michael and Justin Ash, ages 8 and 5."

He nodded, satisfied. That was their past. Now, he stepped into their future.

He climbed the stairs as an exiting patrolman held the door for him. Michael nodded, shaped a smile on his face, and stepped into his brother's world.

———

"Here you go." The desk sergeant passed a telephone to the man ahead of Michael, then turned his attention to the angry man before him waving a parking ticket. The station house was noisy and crowded, the overwhelmed desk sergeant practicing taxpayer triage.

"Lt. Dalton's Office? This is Arthur Griffin, DEA."

Michael looked at the man on the phone. He was of medium height, short hair, wearing a dark suit and matching black-framed glasses. His speech was clipped, intense, every word an accusation.

He watched Arthur Griffin's face redden as he looked at his watch.

"I've got ten to six," he responded. "When did Dalton clock out for the D.A.?" Griffin didn't wait for an answer. "Forget it. Give me Detective Trainor."

It took a beat for Michael to register Detective Trainor as his brother.

"Where the hell is he?" Griffin demanded, growing more irritated. "Is this what you guys do when you blow a case? Take a vacation day?" Griffin shook off the response. "No, I don't want his partner. I have a meeting with Dalton and Trainor tomorrow morning. I got to town early. I thought somebody might be interested in doing some police work."

He slammed the phone down on the counter. Michael stood still as Griffin brushed past him, feeling the heat of the agent's anger, absorbing it.

Anger toward his brother.

———

GRIFFIN RETURNED to his department-issued car, a silver Blazer that in its previous life was one of ten cars belonging to a wealthy drug dealer from Long Boat Key, Florida.

He removed the FBI card from the dashboard and dropped it onto the seat beside him. Reaching to put his key in the transition, Griffin jumped at the metallic slam on his car's roof. Incensed, he threw his car door open and stared across his hood at a man who looked as irate as he felt himself.

"You ready to do some detective work, Griffin? Or did all that whining on the phone take it out of you?"

"Who are you?"

"Justin Trainor. You want me? I'm here." Michael opened Griffin's car door and got into the passenger seat.

Griffin was amazed at Trainor's open contempt. *He* was here to read *him* the riot act. Off-balance now, Griffin got back into his car.

"Why don't we meet in the station?" Griffin asked.

"Do you want to hear the truth or the bullshit party line? Where are you staying?"

"The Piedmont, on 59th."

"Did I ask directions? Do you know the city?"

"Yes, I know the city!"

"Then drive."

Griffin eased his car into rush hour traffic, wondering how this situation had gotten away from him.

"Did you check in?"

Griffin recognized the detective's crisp pronunciation. He had developed it himself after listening to orders being snapped at West Point.

"Take your time, Griffin," Michael Ash suggested sarcastically. "It's my vacation day."

CHAPTER 22

Justin pulled himself free of the covers and sat up on the edge of the bed, his breath as ragged as it was after pushing himself hard on the police gym's running track.

In the dream, he was always running. The woods were on fire and he was running, pulled ahead by the hand of another escaping, their bodies barely visible through the smoke. They ran faster and faster, but it was still behind them. No matter how fast they ran, it was only steps behind them. The *Anger*. Its roar shook the flaming trees with gusts of heat and hatred.

Justin's feet suddenly left the ground. He swung in the air trying to find footing in the smoke. Two hands grasped his. There was safety in the sky. He was pulled toward—

Until the Anger seized his foot, then both, and he was pulled back to the earth on fire. He shouted, then screamed as he hit the ground, afraid to turn and see what had seized him.

Someone shouted his name. Justin looked up through the smoke and saw his rescuer in the tree above, shouting his name and reaching down to help him. At that moment he had hope until the Anger engulfed him and he was pulled into its body of fire. The raging flames burned ragged holes through its eyes and mouth.

Justin had woken then, as he always did, heart pounding, pillow soaked in perspiration.

"It's very clear," a counselor had told his parents when Justin was in first grade. "Your son is running from his past, something he's afraid of."

"And we're pulling him away?" Paul asked doubtfully.

"Away from danger and toward safety."

"But why can't Justin see it's us?" Kate asked. "And this 'Anger,' the fire. I don't understand."

Justin stood at the door outside the psychiatrist's office, his hands cupped at his ear pressed against it. His parents said this man could help him. To do that, feeling foolish and fearful, he had told him about his dream.

Or some of it.

"We have several options here," the counselor was saying. "I can continue to meet with Justin and we can talk more. I can also contact his adoption agency and see if they'll talk to me about Justin's background, for treatment's sake. You can even consider a court order. And there's also the option of hypnosis."

"He was five when we got him. What could he remember?" Kate asked.

"Children often have memories long before that. We can look for them. Hypnosis isn't mental invasion."

"No."

His parents and the doctor turned, as surprised to see Justin had opened the door as they were at his refusal.

There was one more option, his own, that had not been discussed.

In the end, it was his choice that won out. His dreams continued, but he didn't talk about them, to his parents or anyone else. He told them they had stopped.

Problem solved.

———

JUSTIN WAS ABOUT to rise from his bed when he heard footsteps. Quietly, he reached under his bed for his revolver.

More sounds, closer now, deliberate and hushed.

Justin rose from his bed and moved toward the door, his gun extended, gripped by both hands. He watched the bedroom door slowly open, a figure revealed by the glow of the kitchen's night light behind it.

Justin flipped the wall switch and the room was filled with light and a woman's screams. Then a curse.

Bridget clutched her chest, breathless and shaken. "You asshole!" she finally managed.

"Me?" he shouted. "You could have gotten killed!"

"And you could have gotten laid!"

After ten minutes of arguments allaying their tension, Justin and Bridget were in his bed and the gun back underneath it.

"I don't know if I like sleeping on a gun," Bridget said.

"The safety's on."

"No bullets would be even safer. The next time you give somebody your key, you should also give them a bullet-proof vest."

"How did the hanging go?" he asked. Bridget had been supervising the display of her paintings for her first one-person-show at the prestigious Illyria Gallery.

"Do you really think I'm that easily distracted?"

"Talking about yourself? Yes."

"You're right," Bridget replied, stretching out on the sheets.

"Your body is so beautiful," Justin said, reaching for her.

"Thank you, but we're not making love yet. You asked about the show and I don't have a clue how it truly looks. I keep asking for more light, but Alessandra said the gallery will look like a runway. That's not a good thing when you open in two days."

"I agree."

"I think I might have made wrong choices with what to include. Except for your portrait. I know that's right."

"So, I'll be there in spirit," Justin said.

"Don't tell me you're not going!"

"I'm not going! I told you before, I don't know how to talk to those people!"

"Artists? Hello? Do you talk to me just to kill time between having sex?"

"You're different."

"My ego isn't. Ask any artist about their work and they'll do all the talking. You can stand there swigging wine and scoffing appetizers. Invite your partner, Chen, if you want. Or the whole department, a crowd's even better." She swung herself on top of him. "The point is, the only person I really want there is you."

"If I come, can my portrait stay home?"

"You didn't even recognize it yourself, so why do you think anyone else will? I'm done complaining now if you want to make love."

"Okay."

Bridget turned onto her side, face to face with him. "*Okay?* Are we past the 'hell yeah' stage already?"

"Definitely not. And I'll prove it."

"Are you all right?" Bridget put her hand over Justin's, now cupping her breast.

"Sure."

"You don't look it, and I'm not the detective."

Justin leaned back. "I had a bad dream right before you got here."

"What was it about?"

He slid his arm around her narrow waist, pulling her back on top of him. He kissed her, one hand running through her thick red hair.

"What was it about?" Bridget repeated once her lips were free.

"I can't remember," he told her, kissing her again, this time until he truly did forget.

CHAPTER 23

"I PUT HIM IN CONFERENCE B," LT. DALTON TOLD JUSTIN and Chen. "He's been here since seven o'clock. He stopped by yesterday, too, but didn't wait."

"We were supposed to meet today, 9 a.m.," Chen said, on the defense.

"Have you talked to him yet?" Justin asked.

"Not much. Seems he likes us about as much as we like him. Hand the case over, answer his questions, and send him on his way. Keep cool no matter what he says. You know these DEA guys. First they pull the wings off flies and then they break their legs."

———

"AGENT ARTHUR GRIFFIN, Detectives Justin Trainor and Edward Chen." Lt. Dalton did introductions while standing in the doorway conference room. Justin stared at a man only slightly older than himself with a crew cut and wearing black glasses, absorbed in the open files before him. His suit looked a size too small for him.

Michael Ash looked up from the reports, his vision blurred.

Taking off Arthur Griffin's glasses, he braced himself for his first clear sight of his brother. He had been up all night imagining their reunion. Twenty years of dreaming culminating now. He was determined to be brief. A half-hour, no more. Any longer would not be intelligent.

After the beheading of Dr. Larkin, he was certain that authorities were pursuing him. Inevitably, they would pick up his trail once they realized the only person who could be at the end of it.

Michael put Agent Griffin's glasses on the desk and stared at Justin, standing before him. No words. Despite his determination to keep all things logical, he felt overwhelmed. The Justin he knew as a child was here, in this grown man's body. Michael ran his hand across his forehead. His palm came away moist.

Michael stood up. Justin was as tall as he was.

Lt. Dalton was still speaking, offering coffee now.

"No," Michael told him. He pointed to Lt. Dalton and Chen. "You two can go." Michael turned to Justin. "Detective Trainor, stay. Lieutenant, I'll call you when I need you."

He looked up at the clock. It was exactly nine a.m. Michael planned to be out the door by nine-thirty. His hand moved to the left side of his suit coat, touching through the cloth the Glock 17 he had taken from Griffin along with his wallet and I.D.

———

"TELL ME ABOUT THIS CASE," Michael said when he and Justin were alone.

"It's all in the reports."

Michael pushed the files away, looking at his brother, instead. "I want to hear it from you."

Since he had entered the room, Justin's impatience had been replaced by an unease that surprised him. Griffin stared directly at him, his eyes no longer hidden behind glasses. Justin felt he was being scrutinized as closely as his reports had been, maybe more so. Clearly and concisely, he began to outline the facts of the case.

Michael sensed Justin's frustration and ignored it. Instead, he took pleasure in his brother's growing excitement as he detailed the case, impressed by Justin's thoroughness and the pride he took in his work.

An enormous number jumped out at him. Michael was awed by the amount of money that could be made by the man who proposed defrauding a drug company by altering production numbers from the name brand product to its generic copy. Why do people always want *more?* Why are they so eager to lie and steal and cheat the same people they were supposed to be serving?

Michael realized Justin had stopped talking, waiting for his reaction. He knew he should say little.

"So," Michael commented. A word that could lead to any response.

Justin lost some of his confidence.

"Our sting operation to find the man who contacted Kass failed. He cut and ran and we don't know who alerted him."

Michael nodded. Justin searched the man's face for any indication of his reaction to what he had just heard.

Justin blurted into the silence, "So you're here to tell us we dropped the ball. We didn't. But it's your game, now."

Griffin stared at him. Go for it, Justin thought. How will you justify in your report the decision to kick us off the case? Tell me what we did wrong. I'd like to know. I want to know.

"Get your Lieutenant," Griffin said finally.

Almost nine-thirty, Michael noticed as he waited for Justin to return.

He inventoried his emotions. It's ending now. You have these thirty minutes to look back on. Follow your plan. Shake your brother's hand, then leave. Nothing more or less. You've done what you've dreamed of doing.

Justin and Lt. Dalton entered the room, braced for his censure.

"I've reviewed your files and spoken with Detective Trainor," Michael began. "From what I've observed, your investigation has been handled competently."

Both men stared at him, incredulous.

"I commend Detective Trainor's work. It was a pleasure to meet him."

Enough, Michael told himself, you have gone too far.

"I don't understand," Lt. Dalton spoke up. "Are you saying we keep the case?"

Michael nodded. Say yes, Michael thought. Say goodbye and leave the room.

Chen opened the door behind the Lieutenant and his partner.

"Kass just called. They found his wife last night at the St. Regis when a maid turned down the bed. She's been killed."

Chen waited for their reactions to end and continued. "She registered under another name she had a credit card for. They found her naked, no bag, no luggage, nothing to identify her. Kass called her in missing this morning after he tried every hospital in the city. Homicide at the 73rd picked up on the description. Strangulation. That's what they're saying."

Michael watched the men before him as he had watched so many network police procedurals on television. But this show was over. He wanted to leave.

"You want to ride with us?" Justin asked.

Michael paused. He was perspiring. But there was only one credible answer.

"Yes," he told Justin, "I'll ride with you."

Lt. Dalton left the room and Chen glared.

This is not a good thing, Michael thought. Not good at all.

CHAPTER 24

"WE HAVE SECURITY TAPES FROM THE HOTEL LOBBY AND the elevator and statements from the staff. We talked to thirty-five out of sixty-eight guests on this floor. The rest checked out this morning or are returning later. We've got nothing."

Michael watched the detective from the 73rd Precinct bring his brother and his partner up to speed. The police were frustrated, the hotel manager was panicking, and the hotel's head of security looked defensive.

Michael had regained his composure. He was doing now what he was best at, watching in silence. The detective continued talking as Michael looked around the room.

The "Crime Scene."

He had seen hours and hours of crime scenes on television series set in New York. Thanks to Dick Wolf, he was a video veteran of police work. But this time he was a reluctant partici-pant, as he had been once before at eight years old, standing in his yard with Patrolman Owen Moser.

On the bed, only a few feet before him, was a woman's body. He compared it to the picture of a dissected woman in his *My Body* textbook.

Stop.

"What's your take?" Justin was asking him as Chen took a series of cell phone pictures of the body and the room.

Michael had no idea what he was talking about. Again, he had lost his place. Since he had left the station house in Justin's police car, sitting beside his brother in the front seat, his thoughts shifted quickly from present to past, pleasure to panic. Usually, every choice that Michael made, he studied, dissected even, before arriving at a decision. Now he was forced to act and think in real time.

I'm walking closer to the body, Michael told himself. It's my turn to talk.

"She was strangled in his bed," Michael said. Behind his back, he could almost feel the men's patience straining.

"She could also have been strangled and then dumped on the bed," Chen responded.

"But she was found right here," Michael pointed. "That's what you said. Here, in the middle of the bed."

"So what are you saying?" Justin asked.

Michael turned to him. "I'm saying she knew whoever killed her."

"Why?" Justin asked.

"Because she was already naked when she laid down."

"How can you say that?" Chen demanded, the little patience he had now gone.

"The alternative is that the person stripped her when she was struggling or after she was dead. In that case, why move the body to the middle of the bed and put her head on the pillows?" Michael asked him.

"He could have forced her to undress, threatened her," Chen countered.

"And then put her here so neatly after such a violent act?" Michael asked. "That would not be intelligent."

"You think they were having sex?" Justin asked. "The rape kit showed no trace of it."

"Why would he leave his sperm inside her if he knew he was going to kill her?" Michael remembered the initials he was searching for. "DNA. He might just as well have left his phone number."

I'm right on this, he thought, pleased. So long as *Law and Order* was.

"So, she knew the guy, and instead of having sex with her, he killed her," Justin continued. "Then he picks up her clothes, all identification, and leaves her. That buys him a few hours before she's identified."

Almost reluctantly, Chen joined in. "The ME says she was killed yesterday between three and four."

Suddenly, Michael wasn't feeling well. Recalling the case file he had studied, his mind leaped ahead of his words.

"She warned the man who wanted to meet with her husband. And he killed her for it, so he couldn't be identified."

"Slow down! How do you figure that?" Chen was laughing now, but nothing was funny.

"She came yesterday, late afternoon. That was after you tried to meet Kass's Caller in the park. She met him here after it happened to decide their next plan."

"This is total guesswork," Chen protested.

Justin gestured for his partner to stop. "The times fit."

Michael ignored both of them, staring at the empty bed.

"The man in the taxi. You didn't see him well, but he knows you."

"Impossible," Justin told Michael, "I was in disguise."

Michael continued. "He knows because Mrs. Kass knows you both. She sent pictures he took with his phone to identify you. She knew you weren't her husband, and she probably identified your partner. You've met her, haven't you?"

He saw by their expressions they had.

"It's possible," Justin admitted.

"It explains the tipoff," Chen added.

"He has to kill you now," Michael continued. "If he thinks you saw him, he has no choice. He'll be safe then. This is a very bad man."

"A bad man?" Chen repeated scornfully.

Justin ignored his partner, looking at Michael. "I don't know," he said.

I do, Michael thought. I know he'll try to hurt you. And I know I can't leave you now, not until you're safe. I have no other choice.

It was the only intelligent solution.

CHAPTER 25

IT WAS TEN MINUTES TO MIDNIGHT BEFORE HE SAW JUSTIN in the distance, crossing Seventh Avenue toward Greenwich Village's Waverly Place.

She was with him, too. The girl who had come to Justin's apartment late last night. She was laughing. Justin was smiling. He adjusted his grip on the Remington 700 in his pocket.

Otts had a clean shot now of him, but the debacle at the children's park made him leery of taking chances. He was getting paid far better for this job than he was that day, simply as the driver. This was an opportunity for him, for his future.

Justin was coming closer with every step.

Otts debated whether he should shoot her, too. The girl could be an easy target. With the silencer on the Remington, any noise from his first shot would be hardly distinguishable. Justin would fall to the ground. Instinctively she would crouch down over him. Shock would prevent her from realizing he was dead at first. By then, she would be too.

Another fifty feet.

Otts was pleased to see no one else walking on Waverly, before or behind them. Finger firm on the trigger, he prepared to draw his gun.

She pulled Justin toward him for a kiss. Not willing to risk a shot to their heads, Otts waited. They'd move again.

Justin kissed her but pulled back first. He was more self-conscious than she was, the shooter realized. Laughing at his timidity, the girl threw her arms around him.

A flash of movement behind them. Otts sensed more than saw it, but he knew it was real. He looked toward the all-night diner a block away on the corner of Waverly and Sixth they had just passed. A man who had been studying a menu in the window, his back to them as they walked by, turned to watch them.

Otts hesitated, mentally calculating. He had enough bullets for a witness.

THEY DIDN'T SEE HIM. Michael was relieved. He stepped out from behind the corner of the diner he had ducked behind, out of view. He could hear the woman talking to his brother, both now laughing. Michael was confused. His brother was safe, but who was she? Justin met her at one of the coffee shops that seemed to be on every block of this city and they had wandered idly through the Village together.

They liked each other very much. That was clear.

Justin opened the door of an apartment building and they went in, out of his sight now.

Would she spend the night?

Michael didn't know how he felt about that. He realized he had never truly considered the possibility that his brother could feel close to anyone but him.

"I'M LOOKING AT HIM NOW," Otts said quietly into his cell phone. "He is definitely tailing them."

"Describe him," Vincent Krelik insisted, but he knew no more when Otts did.

"He's leaving now," Otts added quickly, "walking north on Sixth."

"Stay with him," Krelik insisted. "Find out who he is and who he's working with."

Wasting no more time, Otts hung up. What he was feeling now was worse than frustration. It was something he rarely felt. Uncertainty. And with uncertainty came loss of control.

Who else had an interest in Justin Trainor, and why?

Otts took a deep breath, centering his tension, then letting it go as he exhaled.

This could be a good thing. There was the possibility there were others who wanted Trainor dead. They might even do his job for him, and all that mattered was that he was able to report Trainor's death to Vincent Krelik. Success was important, a matter of pride and price.

He knew what Vincent Krelik had paid Finn and Chazz for the job they botched in the park, or what they would have been paid. Their deaths were an opportunity for him. Otts had looked up to Chaz, to the point of getting his first tattoo, a blazing five-color phoenix on his right arm, rising from his wrist to his shoulder. He liked the look of the bird and the fire it emerged from. A survivor, like himself.

He took the #2 from Penn Station, then boarded the #1, traveling the subway to 79th Street and Fifth, easily keeping the man Krelik wanted to be followed in sight.

An amateur. He was sure of it. Not only had he bungled tailing Justin and his girlfriend, but he also had no idea he was being tailed.

There was something about this guy's unhurried, almost

casual pace that led Otts to a second conclusion: the man was simply a nosey tourist. He stopped to watch plastic Halloween ghosts filled with helium float above a pharmacy. Stopped to study a diplomat's license plates, and stopped again at a street vendor's blanket spread on the sidewalk like a picnic for hot jewelry.

Still, Otts told himself, there was something about the man's behavior that didn't fit the profile of an out-of-towner. It wasn't until he had followed him to West Eighty First Street and West End Avenue that he realized what it was.

The man didn't look at people. Not once did he stare at the face of any of the countless pedestrians or subway riders he encountered. Like an NYC veteran, the man made no eye contact. Otts noted that he went so far as to avert his gaze. He would take no risk of making personal contact that would link him, even for a moment, to another human being.

It wasn't until he saw his target pass the Museum of Natural History after studying the statue of Teddy Roosevelt on horseback that Otts changed his mind. After waiting for the light to turn, the man continued East into the 81st Street Exit of Central Park.

He was crazy. Or clueless.

Even with his concealed gun and two years of survival training in the Taconic Correctional Prison, Otts would never do such a thing as wander through Central Park at midnight. He might as well stroll through the Bronx Zoo's Lion Habitat at feeding time with a leg of lamb strapped to his back.

Worse.

Otts remembered a pleasant Saturday at the zoo with his sister, nieces, and nephew. They watched, impressed, as cautious keepers fed the lions wheelbarrows full of horsemeat. Even after eating every scrap, they roamed their enclosure looking at their watchers, still hungry.

In daylight, at least, you could see them coming.

But at night?

Otts cursed the man as he crossed West End Avenue to follow him into the park.

He kept a distance on his target, now far ahead of him. He was the only sign of life at this hour except for the infrequent taxicab passing on the Park Drive.

Otts walked quickly past endless rows of benches, lit by lamps that would look equally at home at the turn of the century in Whitechapel, London. Past the dirt. bridle path, over the paved Park Drive and toward a hill where he saw his quarry climbing its stone steps.

Slowly, Otts followed. Reaching the bottom of the steps he looked up. His target reached the top and vanished.

Otts picked up his pace. As quietly as possible he climbed the steps, trying to avoid stepping on larger clusters of the dry, fallen leaves, which would announce his presence.

Hesitating, he heard the leaves continue to crackle without his help.

Otts turned and looked behind him at his target.

"Who are you?" Michael asked.

Ignore him, Otts told himself. He turned his back on the man and continued to walk.

The crunch of leaves followed him.

"Why are you following me?" Michael asked.

"You're following me," Otts called back, increasing his pace.

"You're following me," Michael insisted.

"What are you, a fucking parrot?" Otts was surprised to feel the man touch his elbow. He spun, facing his target only two feet from him. His hand closed around the gun in his coat pocket. He stared at the man's poker face.

"You know my brother."

"What?"

"Justin. My brother."

Otts had his finger on the trigger. Two seconds and two steps back were all he needed

"You want to hurt him," Michael continued.

There was something in his tone that surprised Otts. His words sounded less like an accusation than the voicing of a forlorn fact.

"I don't know what you're talking about," Otts insisted.

Michael pursed his lips, appearing even graver. "You're lying," he said. "You shouldn't do that."

Otts took his first step back, noticing that the man before him was using a stout tree limb as a walking stick.

"You're crazy!" Otts shouted. He backed up again.

"Sometimes," Michael agreed.

Otts pulled out his gun as the branch split his skull.

CHAPTER 26

Detectives Trainor and Chen rode Leon Kass's
private elevator to his Upper East Side penthouse apartment
overlooking the Central Park Reservoir.

A private security guard took them up. A second guard
awaited them as the elevator doors opened onto Kass's foyer,
from which they were led to a library stocked with books that
seemed to have been chosen for the colors of their harmonious
bindings. In the center of the room was a small gym's worth of
exercise equipment that looked better used than the books.

Justin looked out the floor-to-ceiling windows to the land-
scaped terrace beyond. A country estate, he thought, floating
above New York City.

"I wonder where Griffin is?" he asked his partner.

"He knew we were meeting Kass at nine. I'm hoping our
luck holds out and he's gone the rest of the day," Chen said.

"He got us back on the case."

"I'm still trying to figure that out."

"Me too," Justin admitted. He wandered to the library door,
looking across the hall to see a room large enough to fit four of
his apartments. The parlor, too, had a split personality. A large,
flat television screen hung on one wall. The chandelier in the

center of the room was raised high enough so as not to block viewing.

A gleaming modern sculpture nearly reaching the ceiling sat between a pair of Venetian walnut chairs and a 17th Century credenza.

Behold a marriage, Justin thought.

A well-dressed, short man in his sixties, carrying authority as effortlessly as his extra weight came down the hallway toward them with yet another security guard. Flashing a perfunctory smile, he introduced himself to the detectives as Dr. Ronald Freidlich.

"Mr. Kass is resting in his bedroom," he continued. "He called me when he learned of his wife's death. I prescribed a sedative but you should know he has a heart condition. With this kind of shock—"

"We understand," Justin assured him.

"I assume you'd like your privacy." Dr. Freidlich paused a moment, hoping to be contradicted, then resumed. "If you should need me, I'll be waiting in the parlor."

Thanking him, Justin and Chen were led by security guards down the hallway, through a small sitting room, and into the master bedroom of Leon Kass.

"Detectives, please, sit," Kass greeted them. Pale, drawn, dressed in a robe and pajamas, he sat in an overstuffed chair near his canopied bed. Two other straight-back chairs had been placed before it. "Thank you, Patrick." Kass nodded to the guard who left the room, closing the paneled door behind him.

"We're very sorry for your loss," Justin began.

"Who would have ever thought?" Kass looked out his window rather than saying more.

"There are questions now we need to ask you," Justin continued.

"Maybe I can make this simpler for all of us," Kass offered.

"I don't know any more than you do who was responsible for this. You have the names of the two corporate heads I spoke with. I'm fully aware that she was found in a hotel room. I don't want to hear details. She was a beautiful woman, as you know, who was thirty-five years younger than I am. So, I was fully prepared for her to fulfill whatever needs she had outside our marriage. More than giving you a list of all Rebecca's friends I'm aware of, I don't see how I could be of use to you." Kass looked at the men. "I'm sorry. That's all I can say."

A knock on the door. Justin, expecting Kass's security to speed them out, was surprised as Chen to see Arthur Griffin enter.

Ignoring the detectives, he walked straight to Kass.

"Mr. Kass, I'm Agent Arthur Griffin with the DEA. I apologize for being late."

Kass took the hand Griffin offered. "I was just telling your colleagues I have no insights to offer them."

Justin watched while Griffin continued to stare into Kass's face. Not releasing his hand, Griffin covered it with his second, instead. Kass met Michael's gaze with surprise at first, a flicker of annoyance, then a calmness.

Exasperated, Chen looked to Justin. Who does Griffin think he is, a funeral director?

"You loved her," Michael stated simply, releasing his grip.

Kass's eyes filled even as he tried to form a self-mocking smile.

"I'm an old fool. I know that the same as you do. I also knew exactly who Rebecca was and what she wanted. Yes, I loved her, but not in the way you think."

Justin watched as Griffin sat on the edge of Kass's bed, listening intently.

"Do you know Commedia dell Arte? I am *Pantalone*," Kass continued with a weak smile. "The old goat chasing the pretty young girl has always been something to laugh at. When I met Rebecca, I was fully aware of people's perceptions," Kass continued. "But I am a businessman, nothing more and nothing less. As Rebecca was, by the way. We both knew what we were negotiating for."

Kass looked directly at Michael now.

"She brought her beauty and intelligent companionship to the table. I brought more money than she could ever spend and a limited warranty. I'm eighty-two. How much longer will she have to put up with me?"

Kass stopped, realizing his error of tense. "In one way, Rebecca was naïve. She thought herself sophisticated. Of course, don't we all. And she used the beauty she was born with to her advantage. But even so, despite her determination to climb socially, she was at heart an innocent. Because she believed all this," Kass indicated the world of wealth around him, "that this would make her happy. She thought that people who had money were somehow deserving of it, more interesting and worth knowing than people who didn't."

"Did you talk to her, like this?" Michael asked.

"Oh yes. Many times. But she kept thinking there was more out there to find. Our relationship changed over the past three years. I grew more and more fond of her."

"You have no children," Michael said.

"No. When I was younger, I was convinced I wouldn't have time for them. That caused my first divorce. Now, I've outlived most of my friends and find, despite my work, I have too much time. So I was content to have any relationship. Even appreciative. If not husband and wife, then father and daughter."

Kass turned again to the window. Griffin, clearly as moved as Kass, turned to Justin.

It took Justin a moment for him to realize Griffin expected him to take the baton.

"Mr. Kass, I hate to ask you this, but with your wife renting the hotel room and her manner of death, we have to investigate the identity of her lover."

Kass nodded, still gazing out the window.

"We also have to look at the chance that her lover was the man who wanted to meet with you that day in the playground," Justin added.

Kass blew out a breath and turned to them, fully back in businessman mode.

"Detectives, Agent Griffin, I have little doubt now that Rebecca was not only physically involved but in league with him. She encouraged me to meet with the man. She pointed out how much money could be made with the plan he was proposing."

"You knew all this and still set up the meeting?" Justin asked.

"I suspected, and hoped to prove myself wrong. It's why I never told Rebecca I contacted you."

"But if we had arrested him—" Justin began.

"She'd be implicated? Very possible. But we all know money can buy much more than justice."

"You would have taken her back," Griffin said, a statement, not a question.

Kass cleared his throat to say more. "Agent Griffin. The older a man gets, the more the family, the familiar, he was once so eager to avoid becomes a very precious thing. Maybe the only thing."

They were done here, at least for now. Justin rose, thanking Kass for his time and again extending his sympathies. Chen did the same.

Walking toward the bedroom door, Agent Griffin's voice stopped them.

"Wellbutrin?"

The detectives turned, surprised to see Griffin had picked up one of the prescription bottles on the table beside Kass.

"Anxiety? Panic Disorders?" he asked Kass.

"Been on it for years," Kass replied. "It's a stressful business. I've got an ulcer to prove it."

"You should try Paxil," Griffin suggested. "It's as effective as Wellbutrin but much gentler on your ulcer."

CHAPTER 27

For Owen Moser, finding the brother of Michael Ash had become a matter of mathematics.

One hundred and thirty farms within ninety miles of New York City, subtract any not in operation for at least twenty-five years, and the sum was fifty-three.

Moser telephoned Marlene Goldberg, owner of Cherry Hill Farms, on Tom Cogger's suggestion. Mrs. Goldberg vividly remembered not only the county's horse shows over the past two decades but the children who were winners in their competitions.

Were there any seven-year-old boys in or around 1992 she could remember with the first name of Justin or Jack?

There had to be a dozen at least, she insisted. When he asked if she could recall the names of their families, Mrs. Goldberg was insulted.

"Of course, I can," she insisted, naming nine off the bat. Then, irritated that her memory was failing her, she insisted that Moser remain on the phone with her until she came up with five more.

Fourteen boys.

Matching the names on the printout Cogger had given him,

Moser debated if he should start with more phone calls.

"Excuse me," he imagined saying to the father or mother picking up the phone, "does your son happen to be adopted?"

Fourteen calls would bring fourteen hang-ups.

Moser studied his map, circled towns he'd be visiting in Westchester County. Two days' worth at the least. He had been excited to find an actual map in a gas station's shop along the way. A map on his phone would have been too small for his fingers to handle.

Now, six visits and twenty-four hours later, he pulled up the dirt path of farm number seven. So far, the only thing he had learned was that Peggy's Miata was even worse on his back on unpaved roads.

He slowed down at the closed wooden gates before him, reaching from the convertible's low-slung seat to push a button on the metal box beside the car.

Both gates slowly swung open before him.

Moser could no longer risk identifying himself as a detective. Instead, he came bearing gifts: Owen Moser, representative of Fiske-Madden, one of Indiana's largest law firms.

With apologies for disturbing the families he called on, Moser explained that his visit was necessary after the fiery destruction of the adoption records for the Archdiocese of Hatcher County, Indiana.

Monies had been left to Justin Ash by his birth mother, an amount he was not at liberty to reveal until Mr. Ash could establish his identity.

Moser sat then, with one family after another, who regretfully informed him that they never had adopted and never heard of the fortunate young man.

Six out of six families sadly disappointed, but none more so than Moser.

Driving down the dirt road of Bedford Hill Farm, Moser

glanced in his rearview mirror to see the wooden gates close automatically behind him.

Two large barns, a white farmhouse, and a large cleared area set up for jumping, complete with bleachers to watch from. Acres of fenced-in grass fields for grazing. Three horses standing in the shade of a maple tree.

Peggy would have loved this. Horseback riding had always been on her to-do list, along with learning to sign, hiking the Grand Canyon, and owning a convertible she could race down the highway with the wind blasting through her hair.

She got one out of four, Moser reflected. He had bought the Miata for Peggy at Christmas, but by the time spring came, she was already undergoing radiation treatments.

Undeterred, Peggy got behind the wheel, abandoning the scarves she wore to cover her baldness, and letting the cool winds fly across her scalp as she flew down the road. She insisted that she loved this feeling even more, urging Owen to shave his head if he didn't believe her.

That spring, why hadn't he insisted that they hiked the Canyon, studied sign language, and ridden horses until they were saddle sore?

Because by doing that he'd be admitting they were out of time.

Moser parked the Miata alongside the first barn he came to. With no one in sight, he grabbed hold of the car's windshield to haul himself out. Ignoring his cramped legs and back he looked up toward the house, seeing no activity.

He observed the oak trees he passed on the way to the barn. The diameter of their trunks was the widest he had ever seen. These trees were two hundred years old, or more. He had seen numerous historical markers as he slowly drove through town, most identifying events and sites of the American Revolution. George Washington himself might have slept here, Moser realized. Under one of these trees, while his regiment sprawled out under others.

Calling out, Moser walked into the barn to find a dozen horses standing patiently in their stalls. No staff, no riders. Emerging from the barn he spotted a short, elderly Mexican man approaching.

"Hello," he greeted the man, identifying himself, "I'm looking for Mr. or Mrs. Trainor."

"No habla ingles."

Moser scrambled for the scraps of Spanish he knew. "Donde est Senor y Senorita Trainor?"

"Senor Trainor esta muerto. Senora Trainor esta en Albany."

"Albany?"

"Si." The farmhand pointed to the horses in the barn, then to the open roadway in the distance. "Senora Trainor ha ido para la exposicion de caballo."

"Exposicion." A show in Albany, Moser realized. Another two and a half hours from where they stood. There had to be another way.

"Donde esta Senora Trainor's chico?"

The Mexican shook his head no, then left him, walking toward the house.

Good work, Moser told himself. You've mangled enough Spanish to turn the man mute.

He looked up at the farmhouse deciding whether he should try talking himself in for a quick look around in a search for family photos. There was a good chance he'd find some, a decent chance he'd recognize the renamed Justin Ash, and a better than even chance the Trainor's farmhand would call the local police.

Walking back to the Miata, Moser saw the Mexican emerge

from the farmhouse, holding a piece of paper above his head. He walked up the path to meet him halfway.

"Senora Trainor." The man handed Moser a scribbled phone number. "Usted la pue llamar en este numero."

"Gracias."

His spirit lifted, Moser returned to the car, gingerly folding himself back into the front seat. The farmhand stared straight-faced.

"I know," Owen called to him, "I'm too old for this."

"Si."

The Mexican man smiled as Moser pulled away, wondering how much English he truly knew.

He slowed down to push the button for the electronic gates to swing open, then pulled over at the end of the driveway coming to the roadway to dial the cell phone on the seat beside him.

Moser looked through his side window to see two colts galloping across the field toward a huge oak tree, its trunk fenced in so the horses wouldn't eat its bark. From one branch hung a tire swing. Other ropes reached down to the ground tied somewhere in the leafy treetop. The young horses turned simultaneously to avoid the tree, sending swirls of fallen leaves up into the air behind them.

A beautiful place to live, Moser thought, for Justin Ash or any kid lucky enough to grow up here.

A simulation of an old-fashioned phone ringing led to an electronic series of notes from his cell phone heralding an announcement. "I'm sorry," a computer-generated voice consoled him, "Mailbox of caller 914-764-5270 is full."

He pushed the power button, dropped the phone on the seat, and picked up his map.

Red Rock Farm, Pleasantville, less than a half-hour away. Farm eight out of fourteen.

Odds of finding Justin Ash were still fifty-fifty, he told himself. The glass was half full, not half empty. He tried to shake the sinking sense of foreboding he felt. On his worst days, he was fatalistic, on his best, cynical.

Moser pulled out onto the dirt road.

Today would be a good day, he resolved. Driving, sometimes Moser managed to think only of driving.

This morning, he managed it halfway to Pleasantville before she came to him.

———

Two years ago, Peggy's third hospital stay. The day he had rushed to her side from Ash's Hospital, Bunyon Psychiatric.

When her doctor began to speak, Peggy napping in the bed before them, Moser interrupted.

"I don't want her to hear," Moser told him.

"She won't."

"You don't know that."

Dr. James Foster, so young, with his struggling, sparse beard that made him look even younger. They were used to each other. He had learned to meet Moser's impatience with his own unrelenting calm.

"I talked to her on the phone before," Moser began, "she made perfect sense."

"I've told you both there's no point to another operation."

"She sounded fine."

"She's on maximum pain medication. You know that."

"What I'm saying is that she sounded good, not mixed up, like yesterday."

"I'm suggesting that now is the time you need to make a decision, Mr. Moser."

"We both make the decisions! Together!" Moser was shouting now. Dr. Foster raised his hands, palms forward. Stop.

"You're going to wake her."

Moser took a deep breath, conceding.

"There are two options. We've talked about them both," Dr. Foster continued. "We can keep Peggy here, in the hospital, and use the technology we have to keep her body alive. But now that the cancer's spread to her brain she won't be conscious of that. Her body will outlast her mind."

Moser tried to shake those thoughts out of his own.

"Or you can bring her home—"

"Where she'll die faster."

"Where she'll receive hospice care—"

"And die faster."

"She will die, yes. In her own home in her own bed, where you can be with her."

"I can't be with her here?"

"You know you can. And you know Peggy's going to die either place you decide."

"I have to talk to her."

"She's told me you have talked."

"I don't know what she wants."

"You do know. But it's not what you want. Peggy made her decision."

"She's my wife!"

"Yes."

"How can I do any of those things?" Moser demanded. He shouted because he didn't know what he'd do if he didn't. "She's so young! What if you found a cure tomorrow?"

He turned away, wanting to strike out at the Doctor when he felt his hand on his shoulder.

"Cancer of the brain isn't reversible. It's your decision. But try to remember that it's your wife's death."

———

MOSER WASHED his face in Peggy's bathroom, private, thank God, and stared into the mirror until his face looked normal again.

When he opened the door, he went to her bed, looking past the oxygen lines and plastic loops of anesthetics to see his wife. He took Peggy's hand and when she opened her eyes, he almost shouted with the happiness rushing through him.

"Hey," he said instead.

"Hey," Peggy caught her breath. "You again."

"Me again."

"My best friend."

Moser saw how much effort each word cost her. "You know it," he told her.

"Be my friend," Peggy whispered. "Help me."

Moser looked away from Peggy's eyes as they began to fill.

Oh no, he thought, here I go again. Moser turned to the window, forcing himself to think of anything but cancer, but what he heard were the words of Michael Ash, not the sounds of Peggy's weeping.

"There are some people who deserve to die," Ash had said only hours before, "and others who deserve to live. Isn't it the right thing to help them both?"

She's both, Owen thought. Peggy's both.

CHAPTER 28

RIDING BACK FROM KASS'S APARTMENT, MICHAEL SAT IN the rear seat of the squad car, absorbing the tension in the silence.

Heavy traffic added to the stress. Justin escaped the logjam on Fifth Avenue and cut through Central Park, if only for the sense of movement. Chen was a knot of frustration. He took out his pack of cigarettes.

"Could you please not smoke?" Michael asked.

Chen lit one, then turned back to him. "Were you interrogating Kass or making a house call?"

"I was working," Michael answered, riding Chen's scorn. "Next time feel free to join me."

His brother cut off Chen's reply. "You opened him up. That was good," he said as he looked sharply at his partner.

"He didn't let us get a word in edgewise!" Chen insisted.

"We got what we needed," his brother replied.

"We got nothing"

"The cigarette?" Michael reminded Chen. Looking ahead, Michael saw a structure that rose above the trees.

"What's that?" he asked.

Justin saw the direction of Michael's gaze. "Belvedere

Castle. They built it in the late 1800s. Sort of a Victorian Castle with no real purpose. They called it a folly."

Michael stared at a turret, all that was visible. Still, from its height, it would be a lookout over the entire park.

A safe place. A treehouse.

———

BACK AT THE STATION HOUSE, both Michael and Chen were handed messages by the receptionist. Chen glanced at his, then pocketed it. Michael entered the bathroom and read the half dozen messages left by the DEA. They were angry, unable to reach him on his phone. Of course they couldn't, Michael thought. He had gotten rid of Griffin's phone when he got rid of Griffin.

Still, he knew Griffin's superiors wouldn't stop calling. That meant Michael had little time and none to waste.

Leaving the bathroom, he found his brother and Chen settling back into their adjoining desks after getting coffee. He ignored their offer of a cup. Crimes on television were normally committed and solved within an hour.

"I hope we've reached the point where there's a plot twist," Michael stated.

"That's it!" Chen exploded.

His brother called his partner's name in warning, but it was too late. Chen was already out from behind his desk, leaning into Michael's face.

"Listen, you sonofabitch," Chen shouted. "*You* asked *us* to stay with this case!"

"I never asked you," Michael blasted back with equal volume, pointing to his brother. "That sonofabitch asked me!"

"Enough!" Justin said as he came between them. "Let's sit down, take a breath, and get to work."

"That would be intelligent," Michael agreed, all visible anger vanished.

"Let's start with Mrs. Kass's address book," Justin suggested. "We're assuming she knew whoever she rented the room for. We should also cross-reference past and present execs in the pharmaceutical business with a criminal check."

"How do you figure?" Chen asked.

"Whoever could organize a black market has to have been connected to the industry at some point."

It was a good idea. Michael was proud of his brother.

"That's got to be a huge amount of people. Maybe we should ask the Lieutenant for some men."

"I think we can eliminate most of the list very quickly," Michael offered.

"How?" Justin asked.

"You heard Mr. Kass. Do you think his wife would be attracted to anyone who has less money than he does?"

"No," Justin said.

"It's a place to start," Chen conceded.

———

An afternoon filled with phone calls and fiscal inquiries, lists split between them.

Michael listened to Justin and Chen's questions as they worked the phones, writing them down on the pad before him. Adopting their no-nonsense tone, he called down his pages of names, finding most of those he spoke with had no knowledge of Rebecca's death while he asked about their backgrounds and current positions.

Sometimes, ever conscious of his brother's presence, Michael just held the phone to his ear, calling no one, observing him. Late in the day, when he was thirsty, he asked his brother and Chen if they would like a coffee or a soda. Both seemed surprised to be asked.

On his way to the soda machine, Michael passed desk after desk, each seeming isolated, dealing with crime dramas of their own. He walked as slowly as he could, relishing the sound bites from each.

"There's already a warrant out for him / No, this is the wife from Jersey / Last I heard he went into the ministry / Big Greg! It's your old friend Detective Lester. Come see me. Today. I miss you too much."

Waiting in the reception area were a woman with a swollen jaw and a black eye and a teenage boy sitting with who looked like his father, seeming more nervous than his son.

Michael felt jolts of energy from each sight and sound around him, the same dizziness he felt when hospital staff attendants would channel surf in the patient's lounge.

Returning with drinks, Michael overheard Chen apologizing to his brother.

"I'm really sorry to pull out so late. I totally forgot my cousins were coming into town. Tell Bridget good luck and that I'll see her show this weekend."

Justin looked over to see Michael listening. Embarrassed, Michael quickly sat at his desk and reviewed notes as his brother approached him.

"I've got an extra invite to a gallery opening," he explained. "The Illyria. A friend of mine's a painter. It's her show and she wants it packed. If you're interested."

"I am," Michael told him. "Can we go now?"

———

THE BOXER BAR welcomed Halloween with spider webs and masks of horror. Among them, Michael had recognized several past Presidents and superheroes he had seen in commercials. Even on the night before Halloween, patrons were costumed for the parties they were heading to or returning from.

Two hours later, Justin hailed for two more beers. "I was an only child," he replied to Michael's question, "Spoiled rotten. I look back and I'm embarrassed. Just Christmas alone."

Michael stared at Justin, trying to identify what he wasn't saying. Could he somehow sense, from now buried by memories, that he did have a brother? Did he recognize, somewhere inside him, that part of him was missing?

Michael wanted to know. Worse still, he wanted his brother to know. And he wanted another beer.

"My brother was adopted," Michael said.

"Really." A comment, not a question.

Michael sat up straight now, both hands around the chilled mug. He's not looking at me, Michael realized, I'm being stared at but not seen.

"Really," Michael repeated. "Being adopted, that didn't matter. He was still my brother. We were as close as—" He searched for a word, surprised not to find it. His head felt lighter now, buoyant as the foam on his beer. "Blood," he settled for.

Justin was quiet now.

He knows he's adopted, Michael thought. His mother said he knew. But he won't mention it. Why? Is he embarrassed? Is he afraid to know the truth?

I'm the truth.

He drank more beer and felt calmer. This is why people like alcohol. Feeling less is much less stressful than feeling too much.

How long had they been silent? Talk to him! Michael felt as if one side of his brain was scolding his other half.

He noticed sawdust on the floor and as he stared down he felt himself falling.

He had seen such falls. Plunges from a roof through cold night air to the parking lot below. Loud landings.

Tell him, Michael suddenly decided. Tell him who you are. Tell him who he is. Or leave now. Which would be more intelligent? Which would hurt either of them less?"

"Did your brother know he was adopted?" Justin asked.

The weight of what he knew was too much now, more than Michael could carry.

Control, composure. Michael told himself. You've mastered it for years. But now his thoughts were ready to burst from him.

"Yes," Michael answered. "He knew."

"How did he feel about it?"

One word at a time now. "Fine. No, not always fine." Michael caught the shift of his brother's brow. "Confused, sometimes."

"You said you two were close, but what about your parents?"

"What about them?"

Careful.

"Did your brother ever have thoughts about contacting his birth parents?"

Pause. Think. "Yes, he did," Michael told him.

"Did he ever do it?"

"No."

"Why not?" Justin was leaning forward now, keen for an answer.

"I'm not sure," he answered, pulled by the power of his brother's tension. "I never understood why."

You tell me, Michael pleaded. You tell me.

Justin hesitated. His words came from a distance much farther than across a table.

"Sometimes, when you think that far back, it's hard to tell the difference between a dream and a memory."

Yes, Michael nodded. Yes, yes.

"Sometimes I force myself to try. To think back, as far as I can go."

Justin looked at the table now. Say something, Michael told himself. Affirm, empathize.

"What happens when you do that?" Michael asked quietly. "Can you remember anything? Anyone?"

Justin looked up at him and Michael felt himself tensing in anticipation.

"Yes," Justin said, "but they're just moments. Glimpses. Nothing clear, nothing to hold onto. A forest. A house. People."

"People?" Michael prodded too quickly.

Justin nodded. "But I don't know who they are. When I force myself to concentrate, it hurts." He drained his mug and breathed out, considering if he should go on. "No, that's not it," he said, facing Michael. "I'm not hurt. I'm afraid."

———

SHE WAS upon them before Justin could speak, a swoop of hair and a furry coat with multi-colored buttons.

"Here's your tickets," she said, pulling his brother's face to hers to kiss. "Don't be late and don't drink more. We'll do that later."

This is how she talks to him? Telling his brother what to do, forcing a show of affection. Is this a good thing?

She turned toward him now and Michael washed his face of censure.

This was the girl he had seen his brother walk home with. Then, he had seen only a shape. This close, he studied her hair, her eyes, the muscles of her smile. This close she might be thought of as beautiful.

"Detective Chen, you're looking particularly Anglo tonight," she remarked.

"Sorry," his brother said, "Chen couldn't come. Family emergency. Arthur Griffin, Bridget Lee."

She put out her hand and Michael, flustered, rose to take it. "You look like Helen Crump, Sheriff Taylor's fiancée on *Andy of Mayberry*, but your hair is longer."

His brother began to laugh. Why?

"Oh my God," Bridget said, joining in. "You watch too much TV."

Did he? That and reading were the only entertainments he had at the hospital since he was nine.

Smiling, Justin asked him, "Who was Mayberry's barber?"

"Floyd Lawson. He was played by the actor Howard McNear, who had a stroke when the show was filming. After that, he sat in the barber's chair since he couldn't walk and continued to play Floyd until the series ended in 1968."

"You have an amazing memory!" Bridget marveled.

Michael felt proud. "I do," he answered, words pouring out now as easily as beer. "Someone once told me it was frightening."

Bridget smiled. "I hope you don't regret having a good memory after seeing my show tonight."

"I won't," Michael promised. No matter how dislikable her paintings were he'd reflect her enthusiasm.

"Got to go," Bridget told Justin.

This time, he stood and pulled her close for a kiss. "Good luck."

Bridget turned to Michael. "Good luck," he repeated. Michael stood and kissed Bridget with all the enthusiasm his brother did.

Pulling back, he saw Justin staring at him, astonished.

"The fleet is in!" Bridget laughed, then his brother did.

Justin walked her out, sharing private words and laughter, weaving their way through the tavern's tables to the front door.

Michael, still standing, couldn't take his eyes off them. He smiled their smile, in love with their love.

———

TWO BEERS LATER, Justin led him to the Illyria Gallery. Michael was discomforted entering the space crowded with buyers, artists, critics, and friends. All seemed to be talking at once between sips of champagne and the abundant canapes served them. Off in a corner, a trio of singers, using only their voices as instruments, sung what to Michael's ears sounded like upbeat medieval chants.

He looked at Justin. Neither the crowd nor its volume bothered him. He saw only Bridget's paintings, moving in a methodical pattern from one to the next.

Michael walked to the painting closest to him. He was surprised. It was more complex than the simple prints on the hospital's walls. Flowers, bridges, and beaches. Many bowls of fruit. But Bridget's painting, he sensed, was about much more. Colors and images different from real life. Did it mean she was a bad painter? He moved to the next. Again, so much to take in. His eyes bore into it, emotions he didn't recognize filled him.

He pulled himself out of his concentration to look for Justin, who accepted champagne from a server and drank it down with one swallow.

Michael turned back to Bridget's work, now studying a new one. He was especially drawn to this one and suddenly felt a jolt of recognition.

"Guess who?" Justin was now looking over his shoulder and looking as well.

"It's you," Michael said, astonished at the portrait before him. Its subject looked like his brother, but in a way he had never seen him. Far from the frightened five-year-old, the stare of the man in this portrait was a challenging one. He knew things he should keep to himself.

"Finally!" Bridget exclaimed as she approached.

"Everything looks great," Justin assured her.

"They'd look a lot better with sold tags on them," she replied. "Arthur, I hope you're not disappointed"

Puzzled, he thought. "I don't know what to say," he answered flatly.

Bridget looked at him closely, trying to read his reaction. "That's okay, it's honest," she told him. "You can only say what you feel."

"I feel confused," Michael found himself admitting. "How do you *see* so much?"

They were interrupted by two artist friends of Bridget, Ben Coster, wearing a white suit and silver sneakers, and Marie DeLio, her mood matching long black dress. For a minute they talked what he imagined was painter talk with phrases like "Anti-Warhol" and "Emotional Propaganda." When Michael caught Justin's attention, Justin simply rolled his eyes. Maybe he didn't understand either.

Their discussion abruptly stopped.

"He's here," Marie announced.

Michael followed her eyes. Gallery owner Allesandra Dugas effusively welcomed the short, squat man wearing red-framed eyeglasses. She took his coat as he removed his hat, revealing polished baldness.

"What are you drinking, Louis?" Allesandra asked.

"That depends on your show," Louis replied with a smile that was anything but.

Unpleasant, Michael thought, turning to the others. They stared at the squat man with dislike. Justin, seeing Michael's puzzled expression, came closer. "That's Louis Suddeth. He's a critic."

"The only one in this city who matters," Ben Coster said.

"In this galaxy, really," Marie said before turning to the distraught Bridget. "Sorry, sweetie."

Michael almost shuddered. He could feel the rising tension in the room.

"The man can butcher an artist's career," Justin told him.

Michael inspected Suddeth, now even more interested. Suddeth was staring at the photo of Bridget on the wall. Not her paintings, her photo.

Michael saw Bridget staring just as intensely at Suddeth.

"I know him," she announced in a small voice.

"Everyone does," Marie responded.

"No. Not as Suddeth. I know him as someone I met on Match.com. He said he was a writer, said his name was Howard something. He had hair, or a wig. And he didn't wear glasses. But it's him. I know it is."

"When, exactly, did you date him?" Justin asked her.

"Don't pout, big guy. Way before I met you."

Ben pressed Bridget. "How do you know for sure it's the same guy?"

"That, sort of, smile."

"Smirk," Marie corrected her.

"Sneer," Ben offered. "The sneer of a viper."

"That's good," Marie approved.

"He asked me to dinner at Le Bernadin" Bridget continued. "As soon as we sat down he got a call on his cell. He answered it without saying a word to me. No 'I'm sorry' or 'excuse me,' he just started talking on it. And talking, and talking. Not once did he even look at me. Maybe five minutes went by and then I stood up to walk out. I was at the door before I heard him shouting across the restaurant. He still had his phone in his hand, and he was yelling at me, 'I have to take this! It's important!' I said, 'I don't have to take this. And you're not.' Then I left."

"That would be a great story if you humiliated anybody else but him," Marie said ruefully.

"I just hope he doesn't recognize me," Bridget concluded.

Unlikely, Michael thought. Bridget was eminently memorable and he had stared at her photo on the gallery wall long enough.

Tom took a deep breath. "Suck it up, people. He's on his way."

Holding his arm, Allesandra led Suddeth to them. She introduced Bridget, who somewhat stiffly introduced her friends. The critic didn't even acknowledge them, only she was in his sights.

"I don't think we've ever met," Suddeth said to her. A statement, not a question. He watched her carefully to see if she remembered humiliating him in a four-star restaurant filled to capacity.

Michael recognized the tone of a bully. Every statement was a threat aimed to humiliate. The bully hit hard with words, knowing he had nothing behind them but bluster.

Bridget hesitated. She knew the answer he wanted.

"I think we've met, actually," Michael said. "Or at least, I've seen you." Suddeth and the others looked at him in surprise. "Do you go to Le Bernadin often?" Michael asked.

"Everyone goes to Le Bernadin," Suddeth answered curtly.

"Of course," Michael agreed. His gentle manner was gone, replaced by Suddeth's imperiousness "But you remind me of someone I saw there some time ago. Someone ill-mannered, shouting across the dining room at a woman wise enough to leave him."

"Whoever that person was, it certainly was not me," Suddeth flatly responded.

Michael went on as if he hadn't heard him. "The woman put him in his place and left, it was magnificent. Being publicly embarrassed is one thing, but to have an entire restaurant full of people laughing at you is so much worse."

The gallery quieted. Everyone in earshot listened for Suddeth's reply.

"You have a vivid imagination," Suddeth told Michael. "Not the same thing as a memory. Though we agree on one thing," Suddeth's eyes scanned the gallery's walls hung with Bridget's work. "There is no worse feeling worse than being laughed at."

CHAPTER 29

NEW YORK CITY, SOHO.

VINCENT KRELIK'S loft was an enormous space, sixteen hundred square feet of undivided space. At first glance, the space seemed to be an empty box painted linen white. Looking closer, it wasn't bare but had a kitchen, bedroom area, couches, chairs, tables, and a door leading to the bathroom. All were painted linen white.

Krelik never dressed in white, he enjoyed being the only color, the only focal point in the room.

Now, surrounded by blankness, he closed his eyes. Usually, he felt he could concentrate better on the caller in his earphone. Today, he had heard enough. He rubbed a large hand over his face and felt three days of growth.

Krelik didn't think himself a handsome man. His looks were irrelevant. Better that he exuded the power of the man always in control of the situation around him. He felt he spent half his life controlling his temper. He learned as a young man that unleashing his rage, verbally or physically, should be a last resort. What was important only was that those he worked with had knowledge of the few times he did, and the results. Fear was necessary for control. What was even more important was creating an atmosphere where his explosions could be both expected and yet unpredictable.

"Shut. Up." He spoke curtly into his phone. Krelik held back his frustration. What was important was to fix what's been broken, repair it quickly and successfully.

"Otts was given a job to do," he told his caller. "His last call was just after midnight."

"So you think something's happened to him?"

"That should be obvious." Krelik summoned more patience. "Otts was following the man who was watching Justin's building. I was hoping to find out who that is, but I can't wait any longer. I don't like the fact that Trainor and this DEA Agent, Griffin, are working together. I have contacts in the DEA who can pull Griffin back, you were the one who was supposed to do that with Trainor."

"I'm working on that. I need time."

"There's none left. Otts was prepared to take Trainor out if necessary. It is now, and since you were the one who vouched for Otts you can do the job yourself now."

The caller was silent.

"If you can't, tell me now, I'll hire it out," Krelik said. "In that case, you can consider yourself collateral damage."

Krelik would give him seconds to decide before he decided for him.

"I'll do it."

"Good. And make sure it's impossible to trace to us. If they do, I guarantee you'll be as dead as Trainor before they even bring charges."

———

THE CALLER WAS HARDLY conscious of Krelik hanging up on him, any more than the sound of the other phones ringing around him.

Chen pocketed his phone and got up from his desk, suddenly anxious to leave the station house. How could he kill a man he worked with every day for the past three years? Chen realized that the question which mattered most was... how could he *not*?

This wasn't murder, it was self-preservation. He had a wife and twin daughters who had just started kindergarten. Justin had a girlfriend who he was sure would forget him long before he would.

Justin would be out most of the night, at his girlfriend's showing or after-party. He had time to think but knew that the longer he waited the more torn he would be about the decision he already agreed to. If only DEA Agent Griffin had taken the case away, none of this would be happening. Though Chen quickly agreed to take Krelik's money to inform him about the investigation's progress, he never would have agreed to do more. But, now, he could see no other course.

Griffin, you bastard, Chen thought, putting on his coat. He stopped, turning back to his desk. Sitting again in front of his computer he entered the necessary identification codes and accessed the DEA site through the NYPD's network. After a few false starts, he found his way to their personnel search.

Chen entered the name "Arthur Griffin." His department and contact link appeared and then his photo. The photo stared back at Chen. Arthur Griffin, a man he had never seen before.

CHAPTER 30

THE BAR OF THE WHITE HORSE TAVERN WAS FILLED WITH ghosts, presidents, monsters, and superheroes, some of whom Michael recognized from TV. A banner reading "Happy Horrorween" hung from the bar over a framed photograph of Dylan Thomas, and more than half of those present were dressed for the occasion. Even on the day before Halloween, many patrons were dressed for the parties they were about to attend or were returning from.

The Greenwich Village Halloween Parade, only twenty-four hours away, was the world's largest. His brother had explained the event when they passed a team of headless hockey players on their way to the Gallery. The parade was "New York's Carnival," beloved by the city's participants cheered on by spectators from around the world.

Standing next to a gargoyle, Michael ordered another round and heard his brother's voice, speaking loudly to be heard by Bridget. And himself.

"Why did he speak to him at all?" Justin was asking. "He knew Suddeth was a critic. Why would he criticize a critic, and worse, mock him?"

Puzzled, Michael returned to their table. "He wasn't nice to Bridget," he said, surprising them both.

"So?" Justin countered.

"He's a bully." Michael realized he felt unaccountably happy. Was it the alcohol, or a feeling he remembered from long ago, the satisfaction an older brother gets teaching his younger brother about the world?

"Bully's don't stop. They get stronger if you let them," Michael explained.

"The only problem being that he has a newspaper and you don't," Justin said. "It's like you're talking to a wasp and whacking a hive of them as you do it."

Michael was confused. The only way to deal with people was one at a time. It was simple. He turned to Bridget. "I'm sorry if I should be. I thought it was the right thing to do."

"Whether you were right or not, I appreciate it. It was nice to feel I wasn't alone, that someone had my back."

Michael could see that while she was speaking to him, she was looking at Justin. "I was afraid of the bastard, you weren't," she said. "You were angry and acted on it, you expressed your true emotions. I wish I had done the same. I wish everyone would."

Exasperated, Justin searched for a response, but instead searched for the vibrating phone in his pocket. It was his personal phone, not the dedicated iPhone issued to every graduate of the academy. He looked at the caller I.D. "I have to take this," he told them, then headed for the door, hoping the sidewalk noise was less than the din of the bar.

Bridget looked after him. Michael could see frustration on her face. She was annoyed with Justin. Even though it was his brother, Michael realized he was similarly upset, as much as she was. He drained his martini, the same drink as Bridget's.

"Whoa, partner," Bridget cautioned. "If we're waiting for any reviews it could be a long night."

"Reviews?" Michael questioned. "This soon?"

"Sure," Bridget said. "Bloggers can file theirs even while they're standing in the gallery. The media never stops sprinting, everyone wants to be ahead of everyone else. My turn."

Bridget picked up his empty glass along with her own and walked to the bar.

Michael felt the strong feelings Justin had for Bridget. Some of them he understood. Sexually, there was a bond between them. She was attractive. His body told him that. His mind recognized that she was intelligent. Not annoying in the least. But there was part of her he couldn't understand. He pondered that while he watched her wave off an offer of a drink from a man or woman costumed as a man and woman, half of themself as one, the other half the other.

He hardly waited for Bridget to sit down before he voiced the question he'd been forming since he saw her first canvas.

"What you paint... is that what you see?" Michael asked.

"I don't understand."

"Do you see with your eyes what you show in your painting?" He looked for a better way to explain. "Your painting of Justin is not accurate. His face is red. Red is angry. His mouth was small, too tiny to make words. He reached out with his arms but he had no hands. Why?"

"Arthur, you've seen paintings before, haven't you?"

"Yes. But paintings that say what they are. You paint something else."

"That's right. I'm making a painting, not a copy. It's something you don't just think, it's something you feel. It doesn't have to be realistic. What *is* realistic? Everyone looks at the world in a different way. But we're not cameras. We have all these emotions that aren't as easy to paint as the bodies we're in."

Michael considered this. "What you say is coherent. But you go from your eye camera to seeing from somewhere else inside you."

"No. That's my point. I don't look inside of myself. I look inside whoever I'm painting. I want to feel how they feel and think what they think. When I paint, I want to be both of us."

Michael knew he had more questions, but couldn't find them. His thinking seemed slow to him. It took longer to know what was true or not true.

"You are inside them," he repeated.

Bridget, pleased, put her hand over his own on the table. "That's so true."

"Right," he repeated. He looked at her hand on his. He liked the feeling, but suddenly felt too much. His stomach was a blender, mixing desire with a thrilling shame.

Bridget took her hand off his to pick up her phone on the table, suddenly bright with a text.

"Suddeth killed the show," Bridget said quietly. "Me, he slaughtered."

"How?" Michael asked, confused. "He never took a close look at even one painting. How could he review them?"

Bridget nodded slowly. "I feel sick."

"Me, too," Michael said, and then proved it.

———

JUSTIN HAD GONE from the lesser noise of the bar to the deafening pandemonium of the Halloween Parade. He pushed through the sidewalk crowd looking for any place nearby that was quieter. He spotted an alley and went down it, pressing his automatic dial on his smartphone as he noticed a round, yellow emoji taking a leak on the trashcans a few feet behind him.

Fine, Justin thought. He's doing it quietly.

Lt. Dalton never bothered with greetings. "I just got a call from Griffin's bureau chief. They've been trying to get him on the phone for two days now. They traced it to his hotel room, called the manager, and asked him to knock on Griffin's door to give him a message. Griffin's not there."

"Because he's here, with me," Justin said. "I just left him to call you."

"Why isn't he carrying his goddamn phone?"

"I don't know."

"So find out!"

Justin put his phone back in his pocket as he heard a shriek behind him. The emoji was enraged, shouting at the sky in what might have been Japanese, his two white gloves outstretched pointing their middle fingers upward.

The emoji for Halloween in the Village, Justin thought. Perfect.

CHAPTER 31

THE MARRIOTT HOTEL, HAWTHORNE, NEW YORK.

MOSER HAD VISITED seven farms in one day, discovering only that seven more young men were not Justin Ash.

It was almost midnight. Ignoring that, Moser dialed the number he was given for Kate Trainor. Again, he was electronically informed that her mailbox was full.

He should find out what horse event was happening in Albany, try locating her that way. At the same time, he needed to widen his search, moving on to Farm Bureaus in Connecticut, Pennsylvania, and New Jersey, all within the sixty-mile radius he mapped out from New York City.

Tomorrow.

Moser lay down on the bed, turned on CNN, and was dreaming by their second story.

———

Peggy, excited, bursting through their front door with an armful of birthday presents from her class. "Best Teacher" mugs, a ceramic apple, and homemade Popsicle art. She was happier than if they came from Tiffany's.

Then they were in Sarasota, Peggy sitting next to him on a pier bench, her eyes more beautiful than the Florida sunset. They talked for hours, planning their retirement. The life of leisure they would never have. Stacks of books for her, fishing for him. Twilight visits to the Sass 'N Poss Bar, she relishing her glass of wine, he his mugs of beer. And each other.

Years before, now, newly married, Peggy crying all the way home from the doctor who told them she could not bear children. That night, he held her in bed, trying to console them both. They had each other. He had his work, while she touched the lives of a class full of children every day, every year. They could adopt. They would talk about it, he insisted, and they did, off and on for years, until her illness.

The afternoon she told him of her cancer she didn't cry. They sat down at the kitchen table, discussing every available option. Finally, deciding on a double mastectomy, the most proactive choice to be made, they went to bed, Peggy falling asleep in his arms. This time, it was he who cried, not for the cloud of cancer that would follow them from today forward, but for his wife's bravery, her determination to defeat the disease, to stay with him. Tears of gratitude.

Jump forward, sitting with Dr. Foster, who had set the course of battle against each relapse, from the complete mastectomy, chemotherapy, radiation, and now the pneumonia that had settled in Peggy's lungs, her body's immune system compromised even as he fought to save it.

The hospital's coffee shop.

"Sugar? Cream, Owen?" Dr. Foster asked as they settled at a table surrounded by brightly colored plastic chairs.

"I'm good," he told him. "Just tell me."

"She's deteriorating. Quickly. Her brain's already compromised and she's on high doses of medication for the pain. She's really not capable of making an informed decision on any of the choices you have to make now. And she hasn't left a living well."

Moser raised his hands, not wanting to hear that again.

"If you decide Peggy stays at the hospital, there's another thing we need to discuss," he continued. "Respiration protocol. Her system will continue to fail her: heart, kidneys, a blood clot, whatever. It's hospital policy to keep every patient alive as long as humanly possible, no matter what the patient's pain levels are or even their mental capabilities. Because they can't tell us not to."

Dr. Foster pushed his coffee away, taking a folded paper from his jacket pocket. "But you can. You can sign this paper. It says that the hospital is not obligated to use 'extraordinary' or 'heroic' efforts to keep a patient alive."

"So I'd be signing her death certificate."

"No—"

"I'll be signing that I don't believe in her strength or her faith or the one in a million shot at a miracle."

"One in a million? Owen. Do you hear yourself?"

"That's still *a* chance and if you think I'm going to sign that away—"

Moser got up from the table. Go back to Peggy, he told himself. Keep her safe. Talk with her. Tell her all of this. No one can tell me she can't be listening.

"Owen, wait. I know this is difficult. My brother and I went through it with my mother two years ago. Sometimes it's the family that won't let go, even if the patient would want to."

But Moser was already walking to the elevator, then down

the hallway to her room. He touched Peggy's forehead, checking for fever, touched her cheek to tell her he loved her.

All the while Moser watched himself in his dream, not wanting to wake up, missing her so much, sick or well.

If he could only touch her again.

Then, even in his dream, he was conscious of someone in the hospital room with them. A nurse? Dr. Foster? No. He suddenly felt cold, his dream unreal, not true to the reality he was reliving.

He knew who it was without turning. Knew the power of his presence and the sound of his voice.

"There are some people who deserve to die," Michael Ash told him softly, "and others who deserve to live. Isn't it the right thing to help them both?"

And as Moser turned to face him, he saw it. He remembered—

———

He sat up in his motel bed, fully awake, crossing to the TV to shut it off with one hand while he wiped the perspiration from his brow with the other.

He paced the room, reaching for the thought, the image now lost between sleep and awakening.

He saw a rope. A noose? No, two ropes, not one.

Ropes hanging from an oak tree in the fields of the Trainor farm, the horses galloping past them. Ropes, a rope ladder, tied to a branch above, hidden from view as completely as the treehouse above it.

A treehouse. His mind searched back now, flipping years, until he stood staring at flames, Fire Chief Charlie Stone beside him.

"Found the kids out back in a treehouse," Stone was telling

him. "Never would have spotted them without the light from the fire."

Moser looked behind him: Michael and Justin Ash, wearing pajamas, ages eight and five. Holding hands, they looked past him, staring at their house ablaze.

———

MOSER SPLASHED his face with water from the bathroom sink. It was three-fifteen. He had slept barely three hours. He recalled that this hotel wasn't more than twenty miles from Bedford and the Trainor farm. He could get there in thirty minutes.

But then what? Break into their home because he couldn't reach Mrs. Trainor on her phone? And all on account of a child's treehouse, one of probably a thousand in Westchester County?

He picked up his phone and, for the umpteenth time, tried Mrs. Trainor's phone. Ringing. Ringing. Then the voice of a sleepy Kate Trainor.

"Hello?"

CHAPTER 32

This is drunk, Michael realized.

That second martini did it. He felt fine before that. Better than fine. But now, even more disturbing than his nausea was the realization that he wasn't in control of himself. His movement, speech, even his thoughts came slower. When Michael entered Bridget's apartment he had helped her off with her coat. The facilities? She pointed him toward the bedroom. Even with his brother and volunteered to take their coats to her bedroom he felt every step become a major decision.

The coats felt heavier. Michael dropped the coats onto the bed and took a deep breath. New smells here: perfume, candles. Girl smells.

He looked down at Bridget's bed. The bed she and his brother laid together in. Not knowing why, Michael reached down and touched the floral bedspread, pulling back as he heard a shrill beeping. An alarm, he thought, he shouldn't have touched it—

No.

Bridget's coat was beeping. He pulled it out of her pocket and saw the name on its illuminated screen. He should bring it to her but found himself looking for the right button to turn it off.

Why did I do that, he asked himself? Because he wanted his brother to talk only to him? Or because he wanted to talk to Bridget, but by himself?

"Are you okay?" she called to him.

Go now, Michael told himself, leave these tiny rooms and crowded city. Leave his brother before he was discovered or, worse, disliked. Leave Bridget and the myriad emotions that filled him unexpectedly. Confusing. Maddening.

He picked up his coat from the bed.

"Arthur?"

Without another thought, Michael dropped the coat and went to her.

———

"I'll call security," the desk clerk at the Piedmont Hotel told Justin after checking his I.D.

Justin tried calling Bridget again but heard her message service tell him to leave his information. She was angry at him. She had to be. He had returned to the bar only to see an empty table and a waiter cleaning it. Griffin was sick, he told Justin, Bridget unsteady. They left the bar, and when he pursued them with their unpaid bill, he saw them get into a taxi.

"Now I'm stuck with their bill and mopping up after them," he told Justin. "That's the policy."

Justin took out his wallet. The cab would have dropped them both off. Upstairs, he would most likely find Griffin, queasy or asleep.

Still waiting for security, the last of his patience left him. He waved for the desk clerk.

"Just give me the room number and tell security to meet me there."

On the elevator's ride up Justin tried to make sense of Griffin's behavior. Why no communication with the DEA? Why his interference at Bridget's show, was he trying to score points with her? He had many questions for him but wondered if Griffin was sober enough to answer them.

Justin stepped off the elevator, spotting a housekeeper taking inventory at a supply closet down the corridor.

He introduced himself, showing badge and I.D., and asked her to come with him to room 1212. After knocking and calling to Griffin through the door he asked the housekeeper to open it. She was reluctant.

"First day he came, he told me he didn't want any service and anybody entering his room. He had a badge like you. He said he was from the government and had files with him that no one could see. I said, okay, fine with me, one less room to clean. I said if you want towels, just ask. But he never did."

Two suited men from hotel security appeared, but the housekeeper was reluctant to use her passkey.

"Open it," Justin told one of the men. Curious, the housekeeper lingered as security unlocked Griffin's room. With Justin leading, the two men entered the room, then stopped.

The housekeeper looked past them and began to scream.

ACT THREE

"The perfect man uses his mind as a mirror. It grasps nothing. It regrets nothing. It receives but does not keep."

- CHUANG TZU

"And the Lord said unto Cain, 'where is Abel, thy brother?'

And he said, 'I know not. Am I my brother's keeper?'"

- GENESIS 4:9

CHAPTER 33

On the bed of room 2197 at the Piedmont Hotel lay a body in a balloon.

Looking closer, the body itself resembled a balloon, bloated and ready to burst. A balloon in a balloon, stretched tight by escaping gasses caught by the two plastic dry cleaner bags tied together, stretching head to feet.

Medical Examiner Michele Quatrain put her hand on Justin's shoulder.

"You want to step outside now. We're going to cut open the bag."

"Time of death?"

"With the air conditioner on high, he held up a lot better than he would have. I'd say two, two and a half days."

Justin nodded and left the room, leaving Quatrain and an FBI agent who wished he had turned up later.

Looking up and down the hallway he saw officers already at work, canvassing every room on the corridor. 'There was an incident in 2197. Did you see anyone enter or leave that room?'

Justin's phone vibrated. He took it out of his coat pocket, seeing Lt. Dalton had sent a text titled "Agent Arthur Griffin." He opened the file with the attached photo. A familiar face.

Not the face of the Arthur Griffin he had worked with, but the face of the dead man he had just discovered. Even bloated and deathly white, he was unmistakable.

As he ran to the elevator, Justin cursed himself, calling Bridget and reaching her voice mail yet again. Last seen by the waiter at the White Horse, she was getting into a cab with the man who impersonated DEA Agent Griffin and most likely killed him.

He had left her alone with a murderer.

CHAPTER 34

Michael had never prayed before.

Over the years he had been in Bunyon Psychiatric he had met many clerics and religious staff who were intent on teaching him. He tried, willingly, with every one of them, each with the strength of their own sincerity. Words were easy to repeat. But although he could feel the intense emotion that powered those words, he couldn't replicate their sincerity. Normally it wasn't a problem. Belief was not involved, just a reflection of the persona before him.

He needed only to feel what they felt with approximate intensity. It came easily to him, an effortless reflex rather than conscious decision making.

But thought invaded his reflective responses when he was told about the God he was instructed to pray to. God was illogical, self-contradictory. In words he often heard in the halls of Bunyon Psychiatric he could charitably be classified as having a dissociative personality disorder, periodically exhibiting delirium. More accurately, Michael thought, he could be diagnosed as having IED, Intermittent Explosive Disorder.

God didn't have one persona, he had many, all activated internally. He could be called "loving" and "wrathful" within the same sentence, the same God who created manna to feed his starving chosen as the God who flooded the earth, destroying all but a boatload of his creatures.

Now, for the first time in his life, Michael regretted he was unable to pray. If he could, he would pray for death. Pray with every burst of pain that exploded every thought he attempted.

He couldn't move. He sensed his head was on a pillow and that his body was beneath thin, cool covers. Michael tried to open his eyes but couldn't find the energy. He forced himself to recall what left him in this state.

Alcohol, much alcohol, yes. Trying to stand up to find a restroom before he was sick.

He couldn't stand. He was sick at the table he sat at. Knowing he should be ashamed. A cab ride to his brother's girlfriend's apartment. Bridget. Yes. Holding to her walls, making his way to her couch, where she was weeping. Feeling his nausea and her sadness simultaneously. Putting his arms around her when she leaned into him, pulling her close as she cried as if that would stop her.

He was relieved that she kept talking, he didn't trust himself to speak. She was certain the critic's bad review would brand her as a poseur in the art world, that she had wasted years of her life pretending she had more talent than she truly did.

He became uncomfortable when she began to talk about his brother. More time she had wasted. How many times had she poured all of herself into a relationship with a man incapable of doing the same? Was she only drawn to lovers who were emotionally withholding? Did she expect more than a man was capable of giving her? Justin was one more mistake, the one she would regret the most because she loved him more deeply, trusted him completely, and had fantasized about a future with.

Where is he now, she asked? Now, when she had realized she wasn't building a life, she was simply wasting years, time she could never get back. Justin's absence was proof of that. Here she was sitting with a near stranger, but a man who was truly listening to her, sharing her pain, someone whose compassion was as evident as the troubled expression he wore. Justin thought of no one but himself. Another mere man-boy, just one more emotionally stunted Peter Pan.

Michael found himself responding, the need to defend his brother forcing words out, despite his queasiness.

"No," he said, trying not to slur. "You're wrong. He is a very good person."

Bridget shook her head. "You just met him. You can't know."

"I do," Michael insisted. "He was hurt, over and over again. He was hit, he was cut, he was burned with cigarettes. He had to stand on a chair until he couldn't and he fell off."

Bridget stopped him. "What? That's ridiculous! Justin had the perfect childhood! He was the golden boy of Westchester County! He loved his parents! They'd never hurt him!"

"Not them," Michael said. "His real parents."

Bridget was confused now. Who had the most to drink, Arthur Griffin or herself?

"His first parents," Michael insisted, his thoughts beginning to swim away. "Justin was adopted."

"Adopted?" Bridget repeated stunned.

"Yes," Michael said. He should show her. He had the picture, Justin at five years old, standing behind him. He tugged, pulling his wallet from his pocket. A mistake. Now he felt unbalanced, as if the weight of his sinking head pulled him toward the floor. He was falling, he was face down on the carpet and the last thing he saw was the beige fibers on the carpet his nose was buried in.

Michael didn't so much wake as become conscious of his pain. His head hurt, his stomach churned and he breathed with his mouth open. His tongue taste like someone else's.

The ceiling he stared at told him nothing.

He realized he was on a bed. He moved his hands from under the white sheet, reached up and behind him, feeling a pillow. He forced himself to pull back the sheet. Though he had suspected it from the feel of the sheet, he was horrified to find himself with no clothes on.

Michael felt the mattress shift, a slight motion that slapped his head like a wave of an angry ocean.

He slowly rolled his head to his left. Laying on her side, above the sheet, was Bridget, asleep, as fully and shamefully naked as he was.

Frozen at first, Michael was then filled with self-loathing. His brother's girlfriend. He remembered sitting with her on the couch and tipping off it to the floor, but nothing after that.

Carefully, he slid out of the covers and stood beside the bed. His head felt twice its normal size, the extra space filled with throbbing.

Bridget was still sleeping.

If they had done sex together, he was a bad person. So was she.

He had told Bridget that Justin was adopted. What else did he tell her?

Sluggishly he made his way to the bathroom. A pile of his stained clothes, still reeking, had been kicked to the corner.

He should wash his face. It would help him concentrate. He would rinse out his mouth, making it clean again. This he could do, until he looked into the mirror before him.

Michael stared at a man who looked overwhelmed and queasy. No wonder. This was the person who came to help his brother and failed him instead. The man in the mirror was worse than worthless.

"Tell me, Michael," he said quietly. "What punishment do you deserve?"

The voice he heard was not his own. Michael closed his eyes, gripping the sink, but couldn't shut out what he knew for certain.

They were here.

They'd be waiting for him no matter how long he hid, staring back from the mirror.

Two faces, filled with contempt.

Father's face.

Mother's face.

"How long should you burn?" Michael's mother demanded.

"Answer her!" his father insisted. "Tell your mother. How long, Michael?"

"I don't know," Michael told them, reminded one more time that he was a son who was never enough.

"Forever," his mother told him. "You will burn forever, everlasting."

He could hear the match being struck and put his hands to his ears, turning away from the mirror. His clothes, wet and stained, lay before him. He knew he should be punished for his failures. He would be. Michael had learned to punish himself far more painfully than he had ever been punished by someone else.

That would come. But, now, what he wanted most, was to see his brother and say goodbye.

CHAPTER 35

Lt. Dalton picked up his phone, expecting a return call from the DEA instead of Sgt. Denise Del Vecchio at the front desk. There was a detective without an appointment, wanting to see him.

"He says it's urgent," Del Vecchio said.

"Where's the guy from?"

"Indiana."

"Call his station, check him out." Having just learned of the Griffin debacle, Dalton was taking no chances.

———

Seated in the waiting room, Owen watched the receptionist put down her phone.

"I need to see your I.D. again."

He rose from the chair and handed it to her. One call to his former station house and he would not only be found out but possibly detained for posing as an active policeman.

"I'm going out for some coffee. Want one?" he asked.

"We've got a pot down the hall," she said.

"If it's anything like ours, that's why I'm going out," Moser said, smiling. "I need something drinkable. Can I bring you one?"

She agreed and he left the station. He had tried earlier to find Justin's phone number or address without success. Moser ran through the friends in the force he could still call for a favor and found the list even shorter than he expected.

CHAPTER 36

JUSTIN POUNDED ON BRIDGET'S DOOR, HARDER THAN HE did the first two times. He listened for movement, and, not hearing it, stepped back to kick the door in.

That's when it opened. Bridget, with a sheet wrapped around her. He reached out for her, gripping both her arms.

"You're okay?" he asked.

She was clearly hungover and stared at him as if trying to decode his words. Justin exhaled, realizing he had been holding his breath. She was safe.

It was then, looking over her shoulder, he saw a man's jacket crumpled on the couch. Justin immediately reached for his gun.

"Is he here?"

"Who?"

He had already moved past her, looking through the two open doors facing him. Within a few steps, he was in the bedroom. The bedroom was empty.

Bridget began to speak but stopped. She knew Griffin had stayed. She had helped him undress, taking the clothes he had soiled being sick. She had led Griffin to the shower, where he discarded the rest of his clothes and stood under the stream of water once she found it safely warm. She would wash the clothes—

"What's this?"

Justin, coming out of the bathroom, held a pair of pants. He didn't wait for an answer, just crossed to the small kitchen, seeing it unoccupied.

He turned to face her, still holding the pants. "Griffin's?"

She couldn't tell what he was thinking, but that wasn't anything she hadn't felt many times before.

"His clothes are here, where's he?" Justin asked.

He didn't wait for an answer, but walked into her bedroom, picking up a man's watch from the bedside table.

"You slept with him," Justin said. It wasn't a question.

"No!" she answered. "Well, not that way. We both had way too much to drink and—"

But Justin had already passed her, his hand on the doorknob.

"Don't you walk out on me!"

Angry himself, he was surprised to hear the anger in her voice.

"Why didn't you tell me?" she continued.

"Tell you what?"

"That you're adopted! You told Griffin but not me?"

For the first time, she could read on Justin's face what he was feeling. Surprise, confusion, and then a return to the stoniness she was used to.

"Keep the door locked," he said before slamming it after him.

Bridget's head felt as if Justin had slammed it instead. She yanked the door open and shouted down the corridor, even though he had already turned the corner and vanished.

"DID YOU READ MY REVIEWS?"

Going back in, she closed her door and locked it. It felt good to scream at someone.

She didn't want to be done yet.

Something on her carpet caught Bridget's eye and she walked to scoop it up.

A wallet. It had to be Griffin's. A newspaper clipping encased in plastic stuck out from it. She pulled it out completely.

Two young boys standing beside each other, both smiling for the camera. Their expressions were similar enough to suggest they were related.

The caption beneath the photo confirmed it: Michael and Justin Ash.

CHAPTER 37

Chen knocked on the door of his partner's apartment three times before picking the lock.

"Justin?" Chen called out as he entered, just to be on the safe side. "It's me."

Again, silence.

He closed the door behind him as the phone in his coat pocket rang. Recognizing Krelik's caller I.D., Chen answered, getting straight to his news.

"Griffin's not Griffin," he began. "I don't know who he is yet, but he's no DEA Agent."

"Where is he? Where's Trainor?" Krelik asked.

"I don't know."

"You don't know very much."

"They're not at the station, I just tried there. I'm at Trainor's apartment. He's got to show up here sooner or later. Maybe with Griffin."

Chen waited for Krelik to speak. Time was running out, Krelik knew that. He had to deal with Trainor immediately, the only man who could possibly connect him to Leon Kass. Trainor's death was a necessity. Griffin, for now, was just a curiosity.

"You have one priority," Krelik told Chen.

"I know that."

"Can you do it?" Krelik waited for his answer.

"I can do it because I have to."

"Don't think. Just pull the trigger."

This time Chen was the one to end the call.

A tremble ran through him. Was it fear or anger? Not that it mattered. What mattered is that he needed to save his family from losing their breadwinner. What mattered was that, after his partner's death, he would be alive to hug his wife and his girls and never get himself in such a hellish situation again.

Chen took one of the two chairs at the small kitchen table and pulled it across the room. He could see anyone entering, but he was out of their vision until they were a full target. He pulled out his revolver, making sure the safety was off.

A shrill buzzing cut through the apartment.

Chen jumped up, recognizing the sound of an alarm clock before realizing how close he had come to shooting himself.

Walking toward Justin's room, he returned his Glock to its holster.

The room was dark, shades drawn. All he could see were the glowing red numbers of the alarm. He slid his hand up and down against the room's wall searching for a light switch.

None.

Chen walked toward the still buzzing clock, nearly knocking a lamp off the nightstand before turning it on, then locating the right button to stop the alarm. Satisfied, he turned, startled to see a man standing motionless in the corner.

"Griffin!" Chen had stepped back, bumping into the bed frame.

"You know I'm not Griffin," Michael reproached him. "I've just got his gun."

Chen stared at the revolver pointed at his chest.

"Put the gun down," Chen began, but Michael looked at him curiously.

"That would not be intelligent. If I did that you would take out your gun and I'd be the one in danger."

"You can't shoot a policeman! Are you out of your mind?" Chen asked, his voice rising.

"That's not important," Michael said. He gestured with his gun toward the living room. "Walk slowly. Hands locked behind your head. You've seen it on TV."

Michael walked a distance behind Chen, gun extended. He had watched this work successfully on dozens of crime series and films. The only trouble came when the person giving orders was fooled into getting too close so that he couldn't shoot his enemy before he turned on him.

Taking a man's gun away was trickier. He knew Chen carried one but decided not to risk it. Standing across the living room from him, Michael knew he could safely pull his trigger at Chen's flicker of movement.

Chen stared at him waiting for his next instruction.

"Tell me," Michael asked, "who wants you to kill my brother?"

Chen thought he couldn't have heard correctly. Then he abruptly understood. Trying to buy time, he said, "Your brother?"

Michael ignored his question. "Who were you talking on the phone with?"

"The station house."

"No. You said you had already called the station house. Don't lie again."

"Does Justin know?" Chen asked. "Does he know you're brothers?"

"You didn't answer me. Who wants to hurt him?"

"I have a wife and two kids. Twin girls," Chen told

Michael. He felt a sinking in his gut. Justin' brother's expression didn't change. Whatever he chose to do with him would be a decision unanchored by emotion. Which answer could he give that would keep him alive the longest?

Michael's eyes were on Chen as intently as Chen's were on Michael's gun.

"Maybe we can help each other," Chen suggested, eager now. "I'll give you the man who wants your brother and you'll let me walk."

Michael continued to stare.

"I'll tell you the truth," Chen insisted. "I swear I will."

No response.

"You've met him," Chen added. "Lt. Dalton. Justin has proof he's dirty and he's ready to come out with it. Dalton can't let that happen. Put the gun down and I'll tell you more."

Michael hesitated, then took a breath, decision made. "You're lying."

Chen sprang at him, smashing him into the wall as Michael's s shot went wild. The two men fell to the floor, struggling as they grabbed for their weapons when the sound of a gunshot froze both men. A second, a third shot, and the front door was kicked in, its locks shot out.

"Don't move!"

From the floor, Michael and Chen looked up at Owen Moser.

"Lose the guns," Moser demanded. "Leave them on the floor and stand up."

They hesitated.

"Now," Moser insisted. "Slowly. Do it now."

Michael rose and dropped his revolver. It hit the floor at the same time Chen fired his, just a beat ahead of Moser.

Chen fell back against the wall. He put both hands over the redness spreading on his shirt where Moser's bullet had entered his chest. Chen gulped air. Michael watched as Chen's legs gave out and he slid to the floor. He was most likely shot through the left pleural cavity, he decided. A punctured lung only inches above his heart. Was that fatal? He'd have to open his chest to see.

Michael turned his attention to Moser, who held his gun in his left hand, clutching his left shoulder with his right.

"Detective. You've been shot below your clavicle, through your pectoralis major or minor muscles," Michael told him. Weaponless, he approached him. Moser awkwardly raised his gun but Michael ignored it. He wished he had time to cut into Moser to see the bullet's track, but that was impossible. Instead, he raised his right hand and pushed hard against Moser's upper breast.

Moser groaned, collapsing before him.

Michael nodded, satisfied. "The pectoralis major. You'll live."

CHAPTER 38

"Detective Moser?"

Moser heard his name called and struggled back to consciousness. Opening his eyes, he looked up at Michael Ash. "You saved my life, Detective," Michael said. "It's the second time you helped me."

What are you talking about, Moser wanted to ask but felt the rush of pain from his bullet wound and the tight ropes that bound him to the kitchen chair. He glanced across the room. Chen sat on the floor, leaning against the wall, eyes closed, breathing too quickly. The floor was wet around him. How much blood can he afford to lose, Moser wondered?

He fought the queasiness rising within him.

"Detective? You knew I pushed Benny Weill from the roof. You put my board back under my mattress, didn't you?"

Moser didn't answer. If he admitted to it he'd have to ask himself why, for the thousandth time.

He was exhausted, physically and emotionally, as he went back and forth from the job to his wife's hospital bed. He wasn't thinking straight. He wasn't thinking at all. Was that why?

No. The children he interrogated were damaged, likely to go from drug to drug through a life where every day felt as fuzzy as the day before. And Michael? If he arrested him, what more could be done to him? If it was determined that he had the mental capacity to know he killed Weill he'd be sent to prison. Was that all so different than spending the rest of his life at Bunyon Psychiatric?

He hadn't counted on Michael being released. He didn't look that far ahead, or choose to.

Or was Moser's decision made that very day, as he sat down with Michael in the arts and crafts room? When he asked about Peggy, who taught him. Peggy, who got angry with him when he once used the word "monster" to describe Michael Ash.

"There are bad people who deserve to die," Michael had said. "And good people, like Mrs. Moser, who deserve to live. Isn't it the right thing to help them both?"

Because of those words, he had slipped the murder weapon back under Michael's bed.

Moser had agreed with Michael. He still did. Peggy wouldn't accept the idea that there was no good in Michael. Was she right?

"I'm glad I can thank you now, Detective."

"Thank me?" Moser answered. "By tying me up? Let me go if you want to thank me."

Michael continued as if he hadn't been interrupted. "I was sorry to read about your wife's death. I know how much you cared for her."

Moser couldn't bear to listen to him talk about Peggy. "You killed Dr. Larkin."

"I did. He would have fired Dr. Cherry for helping me. That wasn't right."

"Killing him was?"

"You found me," Michael said, bypassing the question. "You're very good at your job. That's why I can't let you go. You'd find me again before I can go away."

"You've got to call an ambulance, Michael," Moser said. He nodded toward Chen, sucking in deep, wet breaths. "That man's going to die."

"He might," Michael agreed, unconcerned.

A phone was ringing. Chen's. Michael went to him, finding the phone in Chen's pocket and putting it in his own. He returned his attention to Moser. "I found my brother." He was pleased, even excited.

Moser was amazed to see it. He had never seen Michael this way. What would have been an ordinary smile on anyone else's face seemed incongruous on Michael's.

"He's a policeman, like you. He's happy, or he was. I'm going now. Someone wants to hurt him."

"Wait," Moser said. "Call 911. You'll be gone by the time they get here."

Michael considered it.

"We'll bleed to death, Michael," Moser insisted.

"I don't think so. Not you. Chen might, but he deserves to. He would have hurt Justin. He's not a good person."

Michael went to what was left of the front door. "Goodbye, Detective. Try to stay calm. Struggling will make you bleed out faster."

———

Waiting at the elevator were three teenage girls wearing colored wigs, a counter full of makeup, and wobbling on spiked heels.

Michael frowned, holding the door for them when the elevator arrived. Who were they supposed to be? Their clothing, or lack of it, gave no clue.

"What are your costumes?" he asked the tallest of the trio, interrupting their argument.

The girl in a platinum blonde wig looked him up and down, deciding whether he was worth an answer.

"Girls wearing what the fuck they want to."

Michael nodded as the elevator door closed.

Descending, Michael was immediately forgotten as Green, in a carefully torn dress, continued her complaints. "Let's skip your building and go to Christine's," she said. "We get zip here."

"What do you want?" Michael asked.

They turned to him as if surprised he was still there.

Cash," Red answered. "Screw candy."

Reaching the lobby, Michael called to the girls already clicking across its marble floor. "Ladies? There's a man upstairs in A-22 you should see."

"Why?" Red asked suspiciously.

"He's giving out dollar bills instead of candy. Ones, tens. I saw someone get a fifty."

"Really?" Yellow asked. "Is he a perv? It will cost him more than that."

"Maybe he's just crazy," Green said hopefully.

"He seemed nice," Michael told them. "But we didn't talk long. He was tied up."

One shared look and the girls headed back to the elevator.

"Trick or treat," Michael called out as they pushed the button.

CHAPTER 39

LEAVING HIS BROTHER'S BUILDING, MICHAEL STEPPED into a world going so much faster than it was when he entered.

A woman with buoy-sized breasts, bare but for two tassels, strode arm in arm with the Statue of Liberty holding a neon torch.

Michael, frozen in place, found himself breathing deeply to push down his panic.

A chain gang of young men sang as they marched together down the middle of Waverly. Michael noted that their chains ran in and out of their open zippers.

"What are you, a mannequin?" asked Mona Lisa as she stepped around him, carrying her own frame. As she passed, Michael saw she had two faces, the second a distinctively disfigured Picasso.

He was gasping for air now. Michael closed his eyes to avoid the overstimulation that would bring on a panic attack. He had many of them at the hospital when he was younger before he learned to think and not feel. Before he thought to weigh what was or was not intelligent.

He would find his brother. But first, he must find the man who wanted to hurt him.

Michael opened his eyes to see a paunchy satyr and Mickey Mouse, smoking a cigarette, with their arms around Goofy. He stepped off the sidewalk and was caught up in the flow of the crowd. It grew larger on its path toward Seventh Avenue. Policeman and blockades guided the swelling tide. Banners flapped from storefronts, proclaiming the Annual Greenwich Village Halloween Parade. Michael decided to walk west on Waverly to avoid it.

Laughter, live music, shouted conversations. Michael was stopped by a six-foot Mae West blocking his path.

"Hello, handsome." She eyed Michael from head to toe. "Is that a dildo in your pocket or are you glad to see me?"

Michael didn't know what a "dildo" was, but it sounded inappropriate. Still, he felt himself turning red with embarrassment as Mae West's laughter was joined by her two companions wearing spangled bodysuits monogrammed "Siegfried" and "Roy."

"No dildo." Michael corrected her. "It's a gun."

Their laughter stopped. He noticed Mae West had an Adam's apple.

They parted for Michael who kept walking until he heard an electronic ringing from his pocket. He pulled out Chen's phone, read its buttons, then pushed the one labeled "talk." Michael put his ear to the phone and his hand over his other ear, trying to block out the very heavy chorus coming toward him singing "It's Raining Men."

"Is it done?" A man's voice.

Michael hesitated. This could be the man who called Chen earlier. The man who wanted his brother hurt.

"Yes," he said softly.

"Louder! I can't hear you!"

Michael realized he shouldn't speak. If he did, the caller would know he wasn't Chen. He held out the phone, pointing the receiver toward the phone's receiver toward the noise of the parade.

"It's done!" Michael shouted over the din.

For a moment, no answer, then a terse reply. "We have to meet. I'll tell you where."

Disconnected. Michael stared at the phone. He felt calmer now, breathing regularly. He would meet the man, stop him, and save his brother. Simple enough. All was not lost.

———

KRELIK PUT DOWN THE PHONE, then ran his right hand over his bald scalp. To him, it was a massage to the brain, stimulating thought. Years back, he went prematurely bald at nineteen. Krelik was furious. His hair had betrayed him. Staring at his heavily tattooed arms he was inspired. He would tattoo himself a new head of hair. It took nearly a dozen visits to a carefully chosen tattooist, each session ending with countless pinpricks of blood where the ink was injected. Silver ink. He wasn't sure he chose that color because it made his age hard to estimate, or because he imagined himself cold and metallic as a machine.

All through Krelik's life, he had read countless self-betterment books all claiming to know the hidden secrets to success. But Krelik knew there were no secrets. Truths are always simple and, often, embarrassingly self-evident.

Krelik held his beginner's guide to life at ten years old when he sat at the kitchen table of a Pennsylvania farmhouse turning the pages of his grandfather's *Farmer's Almanac*.

"A tree is recognized by its fruit."

"Failure is the mother of success."

"A journey of a thousand miles must begin with a single step."

"Despair ruins some, desperation plenty."

"No one saves us but ourselves."

Pocket-sized wisdom from Ben Franklin to Buddha.

Now, behind the wheel of his Mercedes G Class SUV parked down the block from Trainor's apartment, Krelik watched the man he had just spoken with slip Edward Chen's phone back into his pocket. Taking out a photo Krelik compared the man's face to the face of "Arthur Griffin" in a photograph Chen took at the Rebecca Kass crime scene. Him.

He watched Michael reach the corner, pass the subway entrance, and continue to walk uptown.

Krelik got out of his car to follow. Chances are, with the chaos of Halloween, Griffin's imposter wouldn't be able to get a cab. Even if he did, Krelik could easily tail him through the street congestion.

The Farmer's Almanac had said it best, an anonymous quote that might have dated back to the creation of the universe. "If you want a job done right, you must do it yourself."

Krelik touched his side to feel the knife sheath beneath his windbreaker. He still carried his Taurus Judge revolver, as always, but brought this blade as well. The knife was illegal in the United States, a three-sided blade that caused deadly damage with massive bleeding. It had been developed in World War One by the Austrian army and was still popular for close combat. Austrian's named their knife "Jagkommando." The Human Hunter.

CHAPTER 40

MOSER ROCKED BACK AND FORTH HITTING HIS HEAD ON the back of the chair he was tied to. Any stimulation, even pain, was welcome to keep conscious.

Again, he shouted for help, but each cry sounded weaker.

Moser could see the pond of his blood beneath. A surge of panic, then total weariness. He stopped struggling and breathed deeply, filling his lungs and resting his mind from thinking.

Peggy.

Would he see her again?

Never. He knew that. He had told himself a million times since the moment it was done.

He was no less a murderer than Michael Ash.

He had known what he must do, it was premeditated. He thought about nothing else hour after hour, day by day. He sat by Peggy's bedside, holding her hand, refusing to leave. After-noon turned to evening, evening to early morning. Making a decision, as Dr. Foster urged him. As Peggy had begged him.

He knew what he was doing when he pulled the tube to her oxygen, when he reached out to take her in his arms, Peggy so thin that his arms too easily encircled her. He knew what he was doing as he kissed her, touched her cheek, telling her again how much he loved her.

He knew that wasn't enough now.

He knew he had to prove it.

He hugged Peggy to him, gently at first, then closer and closer.

"There are some people who don't deserve to live," Michael Ash had said, and Moser knew then he would always be one of them. He knew as he embraced her, just as he knew Peggy was one of those who did not deserve to die.

The machines around them began to shriek, sending their alerts to nurses, he hugged her when he heard shouting and the broadcast calling for more staff. He hugged her until Dr. Foster and hospital security men grabbed his arms and hands, forcing him to let her go.

He didn't listen to what Dr. Foster said to him as the room was cleared and they took Peggy's body. He didn't listen to question after question he was asked.

He didn't care if he was sent to jail.

He didn't care when Dr. Foster wrote on the certificate that Peggy's cause of death was a heart attack, not Moser, not murder.

You hugged her after the machines started beeping, Dr. Foster kept repeating. Not before that, Owen. After.

Now Moser slid from memory into dream, into warm darkness where he would never care again.

But Peggy would.

Peggy would care that he let Michael Ash go free. She would care when he killed again.

Still, he could do nothing. He began to feel nothing. Thought seemed as impossible as breaking free.

Moser sensed his body, then his mind, surrender to a peace disrupted by piercing screams.

Reflexively, he opened his eyes to see three bizarrely dressed girls staring and shrieking, and closed his eyes again as it came to him...

This is hell.

CHAPTER 41

"Why kill Griffin and then pretend you're him? What could this guy gain from it?"

Justin's personal iPhone rang and he checked the caller ID. Bridget. The Griffin impersonator got her, he thought, as he returned his phone to his pocket.

He turned back to Dalton. "We know nothing, and this guy's still out there. Does the bureau have any ideas?"

"Just one," Dalton said. "Trying to implicate us instead of trying to find this guy."

Dalton's phone rang and Justin stepped out of his office to give him privacy.

What bothered him most, Justin realized, was that nothing had bothered him about this imposter until his blowup with Bridget. He had felt comfortable with the man from their first meeting and couldn't explain why. There was an immediate familiarity he couldn't recall ever feeling before. He looked for reasons in the present, but, finding none, tried to search his past and sensed his reticence to do so. Why? It was as if a door to a long hallway was closed and he could see only glimpses of the person at the end of the corridor through its tiny window. No matter how close he pressed to the glass to peer inside, he couldn't.

Wouldn't.

Shouldn't.

But why? That was the bigger mystery.

"Justin."

He returned to the Lieutenant's office and could see by his expression there was even worse news.

"Chen's dead. They found him in your apartment. An ambulance is on the way," Dalton told him.

Stunned, Justin was confused as well. "An ambulance? You said he's dead."

"He is. Somebody else was shot."

"Do we know who?"

"Let's go find out."

They boarded the elevator, Justin pushing the button for the ground floor and then swearing as they began their descent.

"What?" Dalton asked him.

"Tonight's the Halloween Parade."

CHAPTER 42

Bridget tried calling Justin's phone again, and for the third time was invited to leave a message.

She knew something was wrong, something worse than having a drunken stranger spend the night in her apartment. Justin had to know about this man's wallet and the photograph he had of a young Justin with him in it.

If Justin wouldn't take her call, maybe Chen would. After a short time dating, Justin had given her two additional numbers for both his partner and the station. She had already left a message to call her immediately at the station, so she had only one attempt left. He picked up on the second ring.

"Hello?"

Bridget strained to hear more through the noise of a crowd and the music booming above it. "Chen, it's Bridget. Are you with Justin?"

Michael said nothing, and she continued.

"Hello? I have to talk to him. Do you know where he is?"

Silence. Answer her or not? Michael deliberated.

"Chen! He can be in danger. We all can be."

Knowing Justin was in danger, she might know more. "Danger from who?"

A pause. "Who are you?" Bridget asked.

"I'm trying to save Justin. Tell me what you know."

"You're not Chen."

Michael had to shout now, a brass band in the parade marching down Sixth Avenue was a full block away but no quieter for that.

"I'm Arthur Griffin. Don't hang up. Please. I can come to your apartment."

Bridget's response was immediate. "That's not happening. I'll meet you somewhere public. Where are you?"

Michael looked around him and spotted a subway entrance up at the street sign he stood below. "Sheridan Square and Seventh Avenue."

"Don't move," Bridget insisted. "I'll be there."

Michael looked around him. Human bats and dogs, a giant puppet President Punch being pummeled by Judge Judy.

He closed his eyes, less to rest them but to block out stimulus, and put his hands over his ears as well. Besides worry for his brother and anger at his enemy, he was overwhelmed by an emotion he had never felt before. He was homesick. Homesick for the hospital, missing a world with less volume and stimulation. A place with doors to hide behind and no demands besides fixed mealtimes.

Now came despair. How could he expect to find his brother or his brother's enemy in this city where so many people of all ages and nationalities smashed together to become an indistinguishable crowd.

What would Dr. Cherry advise him to do? Go to a quiet place, work on slowing down your relentless thoughts. Find a peaceful one that soothes you, and rest with it.

There was no peace here, and he would not find rest until Justin was as safe and as happy as he was before he had arrived.

Now it was Dr. Larkin he saw, and his insincere smile of superiority.

Michael felt his hand tightening around the memory of the ax he had gripped and swung down and down until Dr. Larkin's head became infinite pieces, none of them a smile.

No one crowded him now. He was an island in a sea of wary New Yorkers who put distance between themselves and their potentially dangerous street person of the day, fed with the manic energy of the city itself.

CHAPTER 43

A siren normally cleared a path of cars to allow police through, but the siren on the car driven by Lt. Dalton showed no effect on the werewolves, zombies nurses, or two walking eyeballs before him.

In the passenger seat, Justin deliberated throwing his door open and running to his apartment only seven blocks away. Even then, though, there'd be no guarantee he could make greater progress.

He remembered the figures parade officials had compiled from last year. An estimated two million people filled downtown Manhattan to watch the world's largest Halloween Parade. Twenty-five thousand costumed marchers and forty marching bands streamed north on 6th Avenue, grouping at Spring and Broome to conclude on 16th.

Justin saw the still growing stream of people flowing from a side street to merge with the parade, stepping on and over downed police barricades while Lt. Dalton continued shouting threats into his microphone, amplified by the car's loudspeakers.

Enough. Justin got out of the car, telling the Lieutenant he'd meet him there.

A giant spider crawled up the tower of the Jefferson Library. Marching sunflowers twenty feet high followed a red, white, and blue eagle, flapping its wings over the volunteer puppeteers walking below it.

Even a block away, Justin could see that his street was no less crowded. A police car, fire truck, and two ambulances added to the traffic jam outside his building. He spotted Detective Andrea Rossi as he neared the taped-off crime scene.

"Only one alive," she told him. "Shot and tied to a chair. Don't know if he'll make it."

The siren scream of the ambulance behind them came to life, rivaling the volume of a thirty-piece brass band played by angels and conducted by a devil.

Rossi pointed after the ambulance as it pulled away. "He's on his way to Mt. Sinai Hospital."

The ambulance slowed only when Justin pounded on the driver's window as he ran alongside it. He identified himself and a paramedic reluctantly opened the back doors to admit him.

"We can't stop. You'll have to ride with us," he said.

Justin pulled himself up and in. The paramedic slid over on his side bench so Justin could sit. The wounded man secured to the stretcher before him was past pale and in his sixties.

"Sir? I'm Detective Justin Trainor. Can you hear me?"

A flicker of the man's eyelids.

"Tell me who did this to you? Was it Arthur Griffin?"

The man shook his head slightly, indicating *no* to the only answer that would have made sense to Justin.

"Do you know who did?"

The man tried to open his eyes but they only fluttered. His lips formed the word *yes*.

"Tell me," Justin said. He watched the man open his mouth, but no sounds came.

"I didn't hear that. Try again."

Justin ignored the paramedic's protests and leaned down, his head by the man's lips. As the man attempted to talk in barely a whisper a look of confusion came over Justin's face.

Justin stared down at the wounded man. "That's impossible." No response. "How do you know that?"

Justin started to ask again, his voice louder now, but the paramedic grabbed his arm and squeezed. Enough.

"He's not making sense," Justin insisted, but the paramedic's expression said the same about himself.

The paramedic tried to stop Justin from pulling open the back doors of the slow-moving ambulance and jumping to the street. An idiot. The paramedic slammed the doors closed after him, then heard a sound behind him.

He turned to see the wounded man exerting all his remaining energy to speak to Justin, already gone.

"He's got a gun," he said.

———

Justin edged his way through the paraders to the sidewalk, finding a place to stand in a closed storefront. He looked around himself, trying to get his bearings. Ahead, the parade continued. To his right, the ambulance continued east toward New York University Hospital. He had to get out of this crowd to think clearly. Disco music blasted louder as body-painted dancers came toward him.

The man who was shot is wrong, he thought. In shock, irrational. He had no brother. So why, now, was he so afraid he did?

He felt the phone in his pocket vibrate, its ring lost in the parade's volume. Bridget again, this time a text. Justin read it, read it again, and ran toward the subway stop at Broadway and Lafayette.

CHAPTER 44

The Starbucks Michael and Bridget entered to hear each other was nearly as crowded as the sidewalk they had left, and only slightly quieter.

Bridget listened to Arthur Griffin, who now called himself Michael Ash, tell a tortuous story of secrets, lies, death, and violence without showing any emotion to match it. She, herself, was too stunned to do more than take it in.

"Why would Chen want to kill Justin?" she finally asked.

"He was a very bad person. The man who told Chen to kill Justin still wants him dead."

"How do you know?"

"We spoke. He's calling me to meet."

"Then what?"

Michael's expression finally slid to one of curiosity.

"Do you have a brother or sister?"

Bridget didn't, nor did she know until last night that Justin did. In only hours her world had been flipped on its head and a bad review was no longer a matter of life and death. This was.

"Neither. Why?" she asked.

"It's their job to protect you."

"How can you do that?" she asked.

Michael's response was matter of fact, as if he was explaining that two plus two can only total four. "I'll kill him."

———

Krelik positioned himself on the sidewalk so he could see inside Starbucks without being noticed. The man who called himself "Griffin" was with a woman now, attractive and upset. Ideally, his target would leave the store without her. If not, he knew well that "necessity breeds invention."

But, then, there was no way of knowing what he was telling her or how much either of them knew. Still, he always preferred to be safe over sorry. If they emerged together, he could shoot them both almost as quickly as he could knife "Griffin."

———

"We should go to the police," Bridget insisted.

"You should. Go now," Michael agreed, "and tell Justin..." He hesitated. To Bridget, it looked as if he was flipping through his thoughts like a Rolodex, and when he spoke it was with such deliberation as if each word drained him more. "Tell Justin... I was wrong to come here."

Bridget reached out to touch his shoulder but he backed away.

"Tell him I was selfish. When I stop this man I will go away. Tell him that... I... I will think of him. Always. Tell him—
"

"Where's your costumes?" interrupted a mustached man in high heels dressed as a woman nurse. He sucked from his beer I.V. His friend, a thermometer, joined them, and the nurse asked him as well. "Who are these guys supposed to be?"

Michael pointed to Bridget. "She's an artist."

"How 'bout you?" asked the Thermometer. "Who are you?"

"A brother," Michael said.

———

MICHAEL OPENED the door to leave as a customer cut ahead of Bridget. Emerging, Michael felt a man slam into his side with such force he doubled over. It was then when he saw the knife in the man's hand, drawing back to stab again.

Still bent at the waist, Michael rushed the man, knocking him off balance. Michael stood as his attacker righted himself, ready for his second attack.

"Run!" Michael shouted as Bridget rushed toward him. As he did, he scanned his surroundings. Walls of people, then more walls behind them. Running would be impossible.

Only feet away there was a tan and oiled man on horseback, wearing a cowboy hat, white briefs, boots, and nothing else. He played his guitar as his white horse walked patiently along with the crowd. Even at first glance, Michael recognized a draft horse.

As his attacker leaped forward Michael pivoted and grabbed the horse's reins behind him. The horse startled, causing the unbalanced cowboy with two hands on his guitar to tumble to the ground.

Michael swung himself onto the saddle and into his past. Instantly he was on the back of Gauntlet, the horse he cherished during the equine therapy. Michael squeezed his legs, thighs to heels, into the draft horse's sides. He relaxed the reins so there were no mixed signals to confuse it, and leaned forward as he had seen Roy and Ben, Little Joe and Hoss Cartwright do weekly, hollering out a whoop at the top of his lungs. The horse reared up, the crowd jumped back and away, and they galloped headlong into the oncoming parade.

Krelik glanced at Bridget, stunned at Michael's escape. The roar of motorcycles assailed his ears. An unthreatening, middle-aged band of men fantasizing themselves Hell's Angels throttled their motors as loudly as their rev limiters safely allowed them. At their lead, a short, round, man evoking the fierceness of a grocery bagger, sat proudly on his vintage 2003 Dodge Tomahawk, the fastest bike in the world.

CHAPTER 45

Bumping through the crowds on the sidewalk, Justin walked parallel to the parade at his left, moving as slowly as it was. He tried again to locate Bridget's iPhone with his. She wasn't where she told him to meet her, perhaps she, like everyone else, was caught in the parade's current.

His department-issued phone emitted the shrill beeps that signified a call from headquarters. He looked around him for a quieter place to take it when he heard panicked shouts over the parade's clamor. Screaming marchers rushed from the middle of the street toward the closest curb. Coming at them with surprising speed was a man on a horse, galloping with no restraint into the oncoming parade.

Justin stared as the horse and rider rode toward and then past him. Still, the screams continued, this time joined by the rumble of a motorcycle in pursuit. Though Justin saw the bike's rider, his appearance didn't register. He stared, instead, after the man he knew as "Griffin" astride the horse, and he heard the words the man in the ambulance had whispered to him.

"He's your brother."

Why was it a shock, but not a surprise? He'd had an instant

bond with Griffin, had opened himself to a stranger as he had done with no one before.

He didn't just learn now that he had a brother, he remembered. All his life, he focused on his future. His past was behind him like a door not only shut but bolted. He didn't want to look back. He didn't want to open that door, or even speculate on what was behind it. He couldn't. And now he knew why.

Image after image filled his head, a rush of remembered fragments.

So much anger. His parent's anger. His father shouting, never talking, at both he and his brother.

Their treehouse. Their castle. His brother helped him climb up to it, and together they would watch their house through the branches, his father pushing open the backscreen door, bellowing for them. Listening, immobilized with fear, until his brother put his hand on his shoulder and whispered. "We're safe. We're invisible." And he believed it.

Justin tried to stop more memories.

He was kneeling beside his bed, and he was crying. Something had happened. He was crying and afraid when his door opened that it was his father coming for him. But it was his brother. Motioning for him to be quiet, taking his hand, his brother led him through the dark house through the kitchen and out the back door. They were going to the castle, he thought, but his brother stopped before they entered the woods.

"Stay here," he told him.

Justin watched his brother cross the lawn and go back into the house. Then silence.

He waited, feeling a fear that grew as seconds became minutes. And then a scream, piercing, chilling.

He didn't hesitate, but ran as fast as he could toward the

house, threw open the screen door, and ran in the direction of the shrieks that suddenly stopped.

Thuds now. One, two—

Justin reached his parent's bedroom and stared. He could see the actions of what was happening, but couldn't connect it to a reality he knew.

His father and mother, in bed, without faces, only blood and skin and bones. His brother, standing beside the bed with his Louisville Slugger, raising the bat again and bringing it down with a thump that sent a spray of blood droplets into the air.

Michael. His brother's name. Michael.

———

THE PARADE WAS ONLY a blur on either side as Michael rode through fleeing marchers who opened his path ahead. He let go with the reins with his right hand and reached under his jacket to his left side, which throbbed from the attacker's blow. His hand emerged bloody, but not as much as he expected. He cataloged the possibilities of anatomical damage at the point of the blade's impact. Could the knife have pierced his transverse mesocolon that connected his large intestine to his abdominal wall? There should be more blood.

Slipping his hand back in, he expected the wetness of the wound but touched his shoulder harness instead. He moved down to his holster and understood. It had stopped the knife and saved his life.

Even with the wind rushing at his face, Michael could feel himself perspiring. No matter how fast he galloped he couldn't escape the noises around him which seemed to swell. Police sirens and car horns, the paraders' screams, and the growl of the motorcycle behind him grew louder by the moment.

He knew who hunted him, it was only logical. He had heard the bike's rumblings almost from the start. The man who wanted Justin dead wanted the same for him. No matter what happened next, the outcome would be a death, for one or the other.

What to do? Swing a half circle and meet the enemy head-on?

Now the wail of a firetruck. Michael saw it a half-block ahead as he felt his horse begin to slow. Fear. Michael shifted his weight to his left, pulling on the bridle at the same time. They left the parade, heading north on 9th Street, the crowds ahead of him a wall of screams as they ran out of their path.

Two patrol cars ahead now, speeding toward him down 9th. Michael glanced back. No motorcycle, it had overshot him. But before he turned back it reappeared, turning onto 9th in pursuit.

Analyze the problem. The police cars would reach him before the motorcycle could. He could stop, tell the officers he was stabbed by the rider of the approaching bike, that he was would kill again. The police would arrest his pursuer, he would likely be jailed, and at some point, released. But Michael didn't want him in prison, he wanted him dead. There would always be the possibility of him killing in the future.

What needed to be killed was his future.

One squad car jammed on its breaks, the other swung to Michael's left. Michael rode swiftly between them, leading his horse to turn right on 5Th Avenue. No parade, fewer cars. Only blocks ahead, the majestic Washington Square Arch, framed by the park's trees. Constructed of white Tuckahoe marble, its dramatic lighting made it appears as if it glowed from within.

This was right, he thought, and despite the chaos of the night all around him, he felt no trepidation. Escaping Bunyon Psychiatric, the deaths of Bennie Weill, Dr. Larkin, Arthur

Griffin, and Detective Chen were all left behind him. All was happening because it should. Michael galloped faster, then faster still, toward what he knew would be an ending.

CHAPTER 46

"Justin!"

He felt Bridget tugging at his arm, and realized they were blocking the irritated crowds on the sidewalk.

Yes. Justin knew what Bridget was telling him about his brother, but in his backlash of memories hadn't given a thought to the man on the motorcycle pursuing him.

"He tried to kill him!" Bridget said. "We have to find them!"

A voice from Justin's police phone, which broadcast without being caller activated.

"10-29. All cars, alert. Sector 3."

"That's him," he told Bridget. "That's Michael."

———

Wally Norris looked down to remind himself what his Halloween Costume was only to remember he never put one on. Oh. No matter, he still had to make his way from Washington Square Park to Port Authority Bus Station to catch the 192 back to Lyndhurst, New Jersey.

He had spent the money he brought with him during a day

of drinking at McNulty's Tavern, where the costumed crush of people made it almost impossible for anyone behind the bar to spot a fake I.D. Wally and his sophomore classmates from Queen of Peace High School had their first drink by 10 a.m., and in the hours that followed laughed, argued, philosophized, tried to draw attention to themselves, and were ignored by women of every age.

Wally didn't remember leaving McNulty's, but there had been talk at the table of going early to the Halloween Parade to get a good viewing spot, and now he had not only lost his friends but all sense of direction.

He was in a park. A near-empty park. One, two people walking their dogs. He could see a children's playground, benches, and the trash barrel he missed when he tossed his empty Coors Light can.

He tried to remember which street would lead him back to the bus station. He had no choice but to foot it. He had no money and got angry shouts and car beeps when he had earlier tried hitchhiking. They didn't do that here, Wally told himself, as he realized he had never hitched in New Jersey, either.

Uber! He had an Uber account. He wouldn't need cash, as the ride would be billed to him. Standing under the Washington Square Arch, Wally looked up and down University Place, searching for a landmark he could give as his location.

The sound of the hoofbeats in his head grew louder. He looked ahead of him to see a nearly deserted Fifth Avenue stretching in the distance. And a horse charging toward him. Wally cursed himself. He had never gotten this drunk before.

But this alcoholic illusion only got closer and clearer. A man was on the horse, and in that hour-like moment, Wally realized that they weren't going to alter their course. He told his body to move, but his body didn't listen.

A blur of horse and a rush of wind. Wally turned to watch

the rider gallop off but saw nothing but the darkness of the park. When he turned back, relieved, he froze at the roar of the motorcycle bearing down on him.

This time, his body panicked with him. Wally found himself sprinting out of the park, past its sign announcing "Quiet Zone" and down the middle of Fifth Avenue. The roar of the bike's motor was replaced with the ear-piercing sounds of police sirens. And bullets fired... once, twice, three times.

Scared sober, Wally would run the thirty blocks to Port of Authority Bus Station, or keep running, through the Lincoln Tunnel and back to New Jersey.

CHAPTER 47

More than a dozen police cars had already arrived by the time Justin and Bridget did. On the four streets that bordered Washington Square, squad cars and cruisers were spaced so their headlights could illuminate the entire park.

Justin scanned the park and heard his name shouted. Dalton ran to his side.

"Where are they?" Justin asked. "All I see is a motorcycle." The abandoned Dodge Tomahawk lay on its side like a gleaming, fallen thoroughbred.

Hearing a helicopter's blades, Justin and Bridget looked up to see the copter circling above the park, adding its searchlight to the mix.

"They're starting a sweep."

"I'm going in," Justin told him.

"Stay back. The Joint Terrorism Squad's handling it. We don't know who the hell these people are."

"One of them is the man who killed Chen."

Justin didn't wait for Dalton's response but showed his badge to the patrolman on the periphery. Bridget was suddenly at his side.

"I spent more time in this park than I did in class at NYU," she told him. "I'm coming with you."

————

AT THE OTHER end of the park, a patrolman tied the reins of a riderless horse to a lamp post. Seeing this, Justin and Bridget exchanged glances. Where's Michael?

They approached the abandoned motorcycle. Was there a spill, an accident? No signs of blood. No signs of its rider. The man pursuing Michael was now just as missing.

Teams of patrolmen slowly walked through the park, determined not to miss a trace of either man.

"They're not here," Justin said, surveying the empty park. Unless they climbed a tree there's nowhere to hide." As he spoke, he saw patrolman shining their flashlights up into an oak's branches. Another policeman did the same to the maple he stood below.

Justin walked toward the Arch. On each pier supporting the arch itself was a statue of America's first president, George Washington. Commander in Chief on one, President on the other.

Justin noticed that carved into either spandrel above the statues were figures of victory, something they were far from.

He looked up to the roof of the seventy-seven-foot construction. Park lighting left it in shadows, giving the impression that the arch could still be rising, but unseen.

Justin saw Bridget disappear around the arch's south side. When he joined her, she was crouched down, inspecting the brickwork at her feet. She looked up to Justin and pointed: spatters of blood starting about fifteen feet from the arch's base. Their eyes followed it to a small, inconspicuous metal door on the arch's south side, no more than six feet high and four feet wide. Painted the same shade of white it called no attention to itself. Unless, like now, the door was ajar.

"You can climb up this thing?" Justin asked Bridget, surprised.

"You can if you have a key. Or shoot its padlock off."

They walked closer. Someone had done just that.

Justin pulled the surprisingly light metal door toward him. Behind it, empty darkness.

"Tell Dalton we found Michael," Justin told Bridget as he stepped inside. "He's in the treehouse."

———

THE LITTLE JUSTIN could see around him was lit by his phone's flashlight. Inside this leg of the arch were walls of rough brickwork, and, at its center, a black metal, spiral staircase. Shining his light upward, he couldn't see how far the stairway went. It twisted into blackness.

Justin began to climb, one hand holding his phone light, his other gripping the steel banister. He could feel its rust and grime. It seemed that it was rarely used and even more rarely cleaned.

Pointing the light toward his feet he could see droplets of blood on the stair ahead.

"Michael?" Justin called. "Michael!"

No response. He kept climbing. Above him, now, there was a wooden ceiling of wide wooden boards and thick beams through which the stairs twisted. The ceiling became a floor when he climbed higher to its level and stepped off the stairs to look around him. This room, smaller than the one at the arch's base, looked to hold only a small pile of bricks, and, beside it, rusted tools of a bricklayer.

Justin called again. "Michael! It's Justin! Nobody will hurt you! I promise that!"

His voice seemed swallowed by the brick and mortar all around him. He waited, then continued upward, more and more blood spots before him on the metal stairs.

He slipped on a spot where blood had pooled. Instinctively, he grabbed at the railing with both hands. He heard his phone hitting metal steps on the way down, and its crack of plastic as it hit the brick ground floor.

In total darkness, now, Justin continued his climb, carefully feeling for his next step while keeping a firm grip on the stairwell. Two, three more steps, and then he felt his foot bump against something that blocked his progress. He reached down to touch a shoe, a leg, a lifeless body.

Michael? He reached forward, touching a head of hair slick with blood. How could he tell, now, if it's him?

A beam of light from above blinded him. He shaded his eyes and looked up to see someone holding their own phone light.

"Justin," Michael said. "Come up. You'll be safe here."

———

On the ground, Lt. Dalton watched Commander Pat McShane of the Joint Terrorism Squad give orders. A circle of sharpshooters took position around the arch. A team of three was assigned to enter the arch on command and rush to the top. A second team readied ropes and grappling hooks to scale the arch and reach its top.

It was Bridget, now, that McShane turned to. "You're sure there's roof access?" he asked again.

"Two sunroofs," she said.

"You know this, why?"

"Because three art students with a crowbar and feeling no pain dared each other to get to the roof fastest. I won."

McShane nodded, handing off the Pyle megaphone normally used for crowd control to the man beside him.

———

ON THE TOP floor of the arch, with moonlight coming through the sunroofs, Michael and Justin Ash could see each other. Though only feet away, Justin felt the distance between them to be miles.

"Listen to me, Michael. There are policemen surrounding us. They're waiting for us to come down, and they won't wait forever. I can help you with them. No matter what you did, let me help you."

Michael looked at him. Justin couldn't tell if he was hurt or bemused. "I don't need help," he said, "I'm the big brother."

Justin stared at Michael, who stood before him. A mad man? A murderer? A reflection of himself, his own flesh and blood?

"I had to see you," Michael said softly. "That was wrong. Unintelligent. Then, when I saw you, I couldn't let them hurt you. They would. I know how much they can hurt."

Justin stepped closer. "You're the one who can be hurt now," he insisted. "I don't want that."

Ignoring him, Michael spoke again, this time with the same urgency as Justin did. "We ran, do you remember? That night. You were in the backyard. I took your hand and we ran into the woods and then we climbed to our secret place."

"I remember," Justin assured him. "He wanted to hurt me, didn't he? Our father?"

"No," Michael said. He seemed puzzled. "Not him. He would hold you for her. Mother wanted to hurt you. She said you were bad. But you weren't, Justin. I was there. I saw you wash your hands but she said you didn't. She told Father you lied, that you were a dirty liar. He sent you to bed, to pray. But she said you needed to be punished, you needed the Lord's fire to burn you clean. That's why we ran. You didn't deserve it. You never did. Not like me."

Michael opened the buttons on his shirt, pulled it off, and turned his back to Justin.

Justin gasped to see the scars and patches of burned and mottled flesh that were his brother's back, his history. He tried to look away, but couldn't.

"They never hurt you, Justin. I stopped them. I gave them back their fire."

Justin turned away, not wanting to hear more.

"Your partner, Chen," Michael was saying, "he would have killed you. So would the man who paid him. Now you're safe."

"Michael," Justin searched for logic, even as he knew his brother wouldn't understand. "You saved me, I know that, but what you did was wrong. You have to see that."

"No," Michael answered simply. "Wrong to save my little brother? Wrong to stop someone bad from hurting someone good? Then what is right? Doing nothing? Letting people who can't tell wrong from right do what they want? People who don't believe in either?"

Listening to his brother, Justin was amazed at his matter-of-fact manner. It was as if Michael was teaching the child Justin once was.

"I know right and wrong," Michael continued. "Good and evil. Look at this world and tell me you don't know them, too."

"Justin Trainor! Do you copy?" The voice of the patrolman using the megaphone below echoed off the bricks as it rose to reach them.

Quickly, Justin moved to the stairwell and shouted down it. "Copy! Stay where you are! We're coming down."

Justin turned back to his brother. But Michael was shaking his head.

"I can't," Michael said simply.

"You saved me, didn't you? Didn't you, Michael?" Justin moved closer. "I'm your brother. Please. Let me save you."

Michael turned away, but Justin grabbed his brother's shoulders, his scorched skin. Michael gasped, stopped. At that moment, the past seemed to catch up with Justin's present. But now, he was the big brother.

"You're my family," Justin told Michael. "That means something. Something as real as right and wrong. You have to go down."

Michael looked down at his feet, almost childlike. As he spoke, his voice lost all its earlier assurance.

"I would do anything for you. But they'll put me in jail, or the hospital again. I can't. I can't go back."

A searchlight shone up through the staircase. Justin knew what would happen. Michael was right. Life in a jail cell or locked away from life in a hospital. Michael stared at him as if he could provide an answer, a happy ending.

"I'll do anything for you, too, Michael," Justin decided. "Anything at all."

CHAPTER 48

"They're coming down!"

Bridget held her breath until she saw Justin emerge.

Justin alone.

"He'll come down," Justin told them. "But he's afraid. Pull back so the first thing he sees isn't a gun."

"He's armed," McShane objected.

"Not anymore." Justin showed him a revolver. "He's admitted killing Griffin and Chen."

"He has no other weapons?" McShane asked.

"Look!" Bridget said, pointing to the top of the arch.

Even with faint lighting, Michael could be seen looking down at them.

The sharpshooters positioned around the arch aimed at their target.

"Hold fire!" McShane called.

"Michael, they won't hurt you! I promise that!"

Michael stared down at them. In the half-light, it was impossible to make out his expression. All below waited silently for his response.

Justin shouted louder now. "Michael! Come down, now!"

A moment, then Michael shook his head. No. He took a step backward, out of sight.

"Oh my God," Bridget breathed. "He's going to jump."

The sound of a gunshot.

It happened simultaneously. Sharpshooters raised their rifles, a flash of movement on the top of the arch, and Bridget's scream.

"Michael!"

Then Bridget, Justin, and everyone present watched for the endless moment it took the body to fall headfirst from the arch's peak to the stone pavement below.

Commander McShane and Lt. Dalton carefully approached the body. Justin stood back, watching them, his arms around Bridget.

"Looks like he shot himself through the roof of his mouth," McShane.

"It's hard to say."

The impact of the fall was as destructive as the bullet had been. The face was unrecognizable.

Lt. Dalton stared at the wash of blood and broken limbs held together by clothing. He noted that the two shoes were now twenty feet from each other. A wallet was between them. Dalton went to it. Getting one knee and took a pen from his jacket, flipping the wallet open. Inside, pinned to the leather, was a DEA badge.

Standing above him, Commander McShane read out the name on it.

"Arthur Griffin."

"No." Justin had joined them. "He's Michael Ash. My brother."

CHAPTER 49

"I put you behind the wheel of my police car when you were three," Owen Moser told Justin. "You can blame me you're a cop."

Justin smiled at the detective in his hospital bed at Mount Sinai. Moser returned it as if he wasn't in a body cast with four separate I.V. tubes running into his wrists from the pouches hung on either side of him.

"Nice of you to stop by," Moser said.

Justin brushed it away. "If it wasn't for you—"

"Please. Everything hurts. I don't need my back patted." Moser was silent then, looking at Justin expectantly. The silence grew uncomfortable.

Justin stood. "I should let you rest."

"How about you close that door instead?"

Justin hesitated, then did, taking the chair again beside Moser's bed. He looked out the room's large glass window with a view over Central Park.

"Why aren't you asking me why I want the door shut?"

Justin shrugged. "It's loud. The quiet's nice."

Moser stared at him for a time before responding. "Justin, you're a lousy liar."

Justin laughed. "What are you talking about?"

"Tell me this. The man going after your brother. What happened to him?"

"We're looking for him. Vincent Krelik. He's got ties to big pharma."

"So, he escaped your brother?"

"We'll find him."

"I know you will. On the autopsy table."

Justin paused before replying. "I don't understand what you mean. I was there. I saw what happened. Michael shot himself and fell off the roof."

Moser shifted in bed, wincing. "Somebody fell, I don't argue that. And you heard someone shoot himself, you didn't see it. From what I picked up from your Lieutenant when he took my statement, you came down from the top of the arch, a few seconds went by and your brother showed himself. Just for a glimpse. Then came the shot, and the body dropped. The body you ID'd."

"Are you saying I don't know my own brother?"

"No. That's what *you'd* better say. Say you were wrong because of the shock you were in. Say you weren't thinking straight. Because as soon as the ME makes his report, he's going to identify the body as somebody else's. Dental records alone will do it. My money's on Krelik."

"Detective, you must be on some strong medication." Justin got to his feet. "I'll come back when you're feeling better."

"You're making a mistake. I know because I made the same one. I never should have let your brother leave the hospital. I nearly bled to death and he *liked* me. You know how many people died because he didn't?"

"I know he saved my life."

"You can't save his. And you can't change him. Tell them now. Tell them the truth."

Justin looked away from Moser, staring out the window to the Park. The truth. It's what he'd been escaping since he was five years old. Justin pulled back, seeing his reflection. His face, he noticed for the first time, had features he recognized on his brother's.

He couldn't think about the truth, not now.

It would be difficult enough to arrive at the simplest decisions, what was more right than wrong.

It was the only intelligent solution.

———

JUSTIN LEFT THE HOSPITAL, happy to be surrounded by the mass of people he didn't know. He had at least an hour until meeting Bridget and was glad for the opportunity to walk downtown to do it. When he awoke this morning he didn't know what to expect from her. She was still in shock when they went to bed.

He had found her in the kitchen. She looked up from the newspaper, handing it to him. Coverage of last night, he thought, and was surprised when she pointed to a letter to the editor titled, "A Critic's Critic."

"I attended the opening of Bridget Lee's exhibit at the Illyria Gallery," it began. "So I was twice surprised when I read Louis Suddeth's review in this paper. Surprised, at first, at his wrongful appraisal of this talented young artist's work. Even more surprised, however, that he would offer any opinion since he wasn't in the gallery long enough to see most of her work."

"Who wrote this?" Justin asked her. "You?"

"Better. Nathan Stein, Editor of *ARTnews*."

"A big fish?" Justin asked.

"Moby Dick of the art world," Bridget answered.

When he saw her they would talk about the letter and the

impact it would have on sales and her career. That would come first, last night's events second. He would tell her what he knew. One thing he knew as fact was that he loved her. What he didn't like was the realization that he needed her. Needed to believe she would always be with him, even if it were only true today.

What he needed most to talk to her about them. He had to talk, even though he was afraid that once he started he might never stop.

The cabin was in the Pocono Woods on protected land, miles from the nearest dwelling. It could just as accurately be called a shed. There was little furniture in it, a table, chair, wooden platform to sleep on, all as weathered as the cabin itself. An ancient wood-burning stove. A hole in the roof as big as a bucket. A bucket on the floor to catch the rain. The outhouse was twenty feet from the front door.

From the dank condition of the place, any hunter that had used this property did so years ago. A hunter today might consider sleeping outside in their tent or even a sleeping bag on the forest floor.

The light in the cabin was provided by candles and the crackling glow of the logs in the fireplace. An easel held a canvas. Brush in hand, Michael looked up from his work and squinted across the room for a closer look at his subject. He rose, rearranged some candles to get more flattering light, then sat back behind his canvas.

There. Now he could better see the head of Louis Suddeth, pinned to the tree stump with ring shank nails. Suddeth's eyes were opened wide in surprise. His face was frozen in a permanent grimace.

Staring at it, Michael's expression slowly changed to mirror it.

He picked up his brush to complete his portrait with a series of thick, red X's across the critic's mouth.

ABOUT THE AUTHOR

MARK ST. GERMAIN has written for film, television, and the stage. His dozens of plays and musicals include *Freud's Last Session, Dancing Lessons,* and *Becoming Dr. Ruth.*

Mark co-wrote Caroll Ballard's film *Duma,* and directed the documentary *My Dog: An Unconditional Love Story.*

Mark also wrote the children's book *Three Cups* and the comedic memoir *Walking Evil: How Man's Best Friend Became My Worst Enemy.*

Mark's work has received the Lucille Lortel Award, the Outer Critics Circle Award, and the Off-Broadway Alliance Award.

Mark is an Associate Artist at the Barrington Stage Company in the Berkshires, where a theater has been named after him.

MORE THRILLS FROM IBIS BOOKS!

Even the largest dog comes to heel...

A brutal dog-fighting ring up in the Georgia mountains.
A secret team of vigilantes with vast resources.
An undercover operation that goes sideways.

It's time to let *THE UNDERSTUDY* off the leash.

If you like Lee Child, James Rollins, Dan Brown, Randy
Wayne White, *Criminal Minds*, or Broadway plays—yes,
seriously!—then *THE UNDERSTUDY* is for you.

Get your FREE copy of *THE UNDERSTUDY* at
ibis-books.com

www.ingramcontent.com/pod-product-compliance
Lightning Source LLC
Chambersburg PA
CBHW050838190726
48286CB00007B/2135